HELL AND HEXES

DEBRA DUNBAR

debra/dunbar
SERIOUSLY FUN FICTION

CHAPTER 1

ESHU

"Where's the couch-witch?" I looked around the living room, even kneeling to check under the furniture. Just to be thorough, you know.

Lucien scowled. "As I was saying, blah-blah. Blah blah blah. Blah."

I was pretty sure he didn't actually say that, but I wasn't paying attention. It was my dubious honor to spend my immortal life as a messenger because not only did the denizens of hell and the inhabitants of heaven refuse to communicate with each other, they often refused to communicate among themselves. Million-year-old fights and the inclination to hold an incredible grudge made my job possible.

"Got it. Tell Boor to give Malias an extra hour in the boiling oil and let heaven know that you think we got this Elijah guy in error. Now, where's the couch-witch?" I went over and looked in the closet, but all I saw were coats and boots. No witch.

"Sylvie went back to her home."

Lucien's scowl grew to the point where I was pretty sure

his face was going to freeze like that. I knew his foul mood this time didn't have to do with business or me, but the fact that his main-squeeze witch was not happy about her sister returning home. Cassie made no secret of the fact that she didn't think her sister was completely healed from some accident, and that she needed the elder sister's continued suffocating attentiveness. Sylvie felt differently, but she also felt beholden to her sister and flattered by the love and care bestowed upon her throughout her life.

See? I occasionally paid attention.

"Where is the couch-witch's home?" I tried to make that a casual question, but clearly failed from the deepening scowl on Lucien's face.

"You need to leave her alone. She's not interested in you."

Actually, I got the impression my couch-witch *was* interested in me. I'd been trying to woo her from the first day I'd showed up to collect and deliver messages and found the gorgeous witch sleeping on the couch in a pair of pajamas with Pikachu on them, her dark hair a tangled mess, drool dampening the pillow as she snored.

But to woo her, I'd need to pull out the big guns. I might not have Lucien's lofty pedigree or good looks, but I had one thing going for me. It was my ace in the hole.

No, not my giant schlong, you pervs. My sense of humor. Although I've been told my schlong *is* a considerable asset. In this case, I went with humor, because I got the idea that pulling my trouser snake out would have been something that resulted in my being fried to a crisp by both a witch *and* a demon, then banished from the house.

Plus, I knew that was not the best way to woo my couch-witch. Humor first, then once I knew she was totally smitten, I'd whip out the grade-A salami in my pants.

I'd made her laugh. And with that first laugh, I'd been lost. What I'd hoped would be a fun diversion took a right turn into Seriousville that would normally have sent me running. I couldn't run, though. When she'd laughed at my joke, her bright blue eyes meeting mine, my heart leapt right out of my chest and into her hands.

Two weeks I'd seen her on that couch. Two weeks I'd come up with any excuse necessary to show up two or three times a day to deliver or pick up messages. I'd never taken my job so seriously in my life.

Actually, I wasn't taking my job seriously. I still gave messages to the wrong people and frequently bungled what I was supposed to be relaying. There was a war in the third circle because of me. Oh, well. It was hell. Not like anyone was actually going to die-die. Not unless the big guy himself got involved, that is.

But now she was gone, and I was completely uninterested in messages and intensely interested in finding out where she lived. I had a new limerick to tell her about a man from Nantucket. I was pretty sure she'd find it so funny that I'd be able to show her my massive pole and then we'd go straight to her bedroom.

At least, that was the fantasy running through my mind right now.

"Eshu! Did you hear a word I said?" Lucien snapped.

"Yep. Tell Bartholomew that Matt needs to get out of the hot tub and let heaven know we've got Elijah and we're not giving him back without a fight."

The demon dropped his head in his hands with so much force I heard it smack. "That's not what I said."

He then repeated what he said. I think it had something to do with a demon named Bob. Hell if I knew. I wasn't paying attention. I was too busy wondering where my couch-witch lived and thinking of how beautiful she was when she laughed.

CHAPTER 2

"*A*nd how does that make you feel, Alberta?"

The troll shifted; her gaze fixed on something outside the window. "Well…"

"Make sure you look at Shelby when you say it," I instructed her.

The troll looked over at the werewolf next to her and her expression softened. "It makes me afraid that you're gonna leave me. Like maybe you think you made a mistake giving up your pack to come stay with me and that you wanna go back."

There. I sat back in my chair as I saw Shelby quickly wipe away a tear. In reality, I was holding back my own tears. This was such a win. Alberta had trust and abandonment issues. I mean, most of us had abandonment issues, me included, but Alberta had a hard time articulating them to the werewolf she loved. And Shelby, like most werewolves, kept every emotion except for anger close to the vest. She'd been sneaking out at night after Alberta was asleep, running on four legs as close to the mountain as she dared and listening to her former pack howl and yip as they hunted or partied. It had taken a lot for her to admit it to Alberta. And it had taken a lot for Alberta to admit that the little passive-aggressive things she'd been doing the last two weeks came from a place of fear and self-doubt.

"I made a choice, Alberta. Twice I made a choice and both times I chose you. It's just…" The werewolf ran a hand through her short hair. "It hurts every time I go up there to listen. It hurts and I know I shouldn't do it, but I can't help myself. It's torture to hear them and remember that I'll never have that again. It's like slicing open a raw wound and digging the knife in deeper."

"Then why?" Alberta's eyes searched hers. "Why can't you just stay in bed with me? Aren't I enough?"

Shelby hesitated, biting her lip.

"A love that doesn't allow room for other things isn't healthy, Alberta," I gently told the troll. "Hobbies, friends, a career—activities that don't include the love of your life actually *enhance* your relationship. They give it strength. They breathe fresh air into a union that might otherwise suffocate."

They both looked at each other for a long moment and I waited, feeling that something big was about to happen.

"I don't feel like I can mourn the loss of my pack with you," Shelby finally blurted out. "You'll internalize it and think it's your fault I can't hunt with them or see them anymore. You'll blame yourself, and I don't want you to do that 'cause it's not true. *I* made the choice. Me. That's how important you are to me, Alberta. I gave up everything for you 'cause I love you and I knew that the life I was going to have with you would be a thousand times better than my life with the pack. But there are times when I'm sad, times when I need to mourn what I left behind."

Alberta's lips quivered. "I'm so glad you chose me. I love you and I'm so glad."

Shelby reached out and took the troll's hands. "I love you too. And until they accept you as my fated mate, I'm never going back. Do you hear me, Alberta? I'm not going to leave you for them. Not now. Not ever. I love you."

"Next time, wake me up and take me with you," Alberta said softly. "Or if you need to be alone, then wake me up when you return home so I can mourn with you."

Shelby was silent for a moment, then nodded. "Okay. I will. And I promise I'll talk to you when I'm feeling homesick and not bottle it up. Just know it's not your fault. I'm not complaining, and I'm not blaming you. I just miss it all sometimes."

They hugged and I watched on in silence, thrilled at the breakthrough.

"You've both made great progress today," I told the pair as I looked up at the clock and pulled out my appointment book. "Same time next week?"

"I think…" Alberta reached out and took Shelby's hand. "I think maybe we could wait and schedule something for the following week?"

Shelby nodded enthusiastically, and I marked the appointment down in my book, murmuring the words that would render my notes indecipherable to anyone except me only to have nothing happen.

Crap. For two weeks, this sort of thing had been occurring—or rather *not* occurring. It hadn't been a big deal when I was recuperating on Cassie's couch, but now that I was resuming my life, my lack of magic caught me by surprise and sent a bolt of panic through me.

I took a calming breath and tried to think rationally. Maybe my magic would return as I healed, but in the meantime, I'd need to learn some sort of code or shorthand or get another safe to lock my appointment books and files up. What a royal pain in the butt.

I pushed down the frustration and fear and presented a composed demeanor as I finished my notes and wrapped up the appointment with my clients. Making sure both Alberta and Shelby still had the charms I'd created months ago for my clients—charms that allowed them to come and go from my office without notice—I saw them to my door. Privacy was so important in a town full of supernatural creatures. No one wanted the gossip mill talking about how they were seen going to the sex therapist.

In reality, discussions involving sex were a minor part of my practice, but it was the most salacious part of my job and thus what everyone thought I spent every therapy session on. I kinda was to blame for some of that. It was so much fun to see how flustered people got when I calmly and clinically discussed kinky practices. Despite that, I was glad my practice wasn't sex therapy all day every day. That would get boring fast.

Most of my clients were like Alberta and Shelby—people just trying to work through relationship issues and needing a little guidance. Other clients were more on the life-coach side of my practice where I assisted with things like a vampire's mid-life crisis, a gnome who wanted to confront his fear of flying, a sylph who was contemplating a career change, or a pixie who wanted to learn better confrontation techniques. In Accident, I was the go-to for people who had problems in their lives.

Which was really funny since my own life was a complete and utter disaster. Two weeks ago, I'd died. And although I'd come back to life, things hadn't been truly right since that night when I got electrocuted trying to microwave a bottle of hot fudge.

I'd died, and my twin sister Ophelia had made some sort of deal with a reaper where I'd been brought back to life. She was now dating that reaper. In fact, he was living in her house in a crazy whirlwind romance that seemed to be how my sisters rolled lately. I was okay with it since Nash seemed like a pretty cool guy, and he clearly loved Ophelia. And I did owe the guy big time for stuffing me back in my body when I should have been heading toward the light.

Shelby and Alberta were my last clients of the day, so I locked up the office, scrawling a hex on the front door just in case some goblin got ideas. I went to charge it, only to feel…nothing.

Crap. Checking the locks, I hoped that any nosy goblins would see the hex symbol and decide not to try to call my bluff. Then once again, I shoved the frustration and fear deep down inside and headed down the stairs to slowly make the four--block walk to my house.

By the time I reached my door, I was exhausted and wishing I'd driven to work. Maybe Cassie was right. Maybe I *wasn't* ready to leave her couch and come back home. But my clients needed me. I'd already had to reschedule two weeks of appointments and couldn't continue to do that. And, I was going crazy on Cassie's couch. She was fussing over me like…well, like I'd been at death's door. I was bored and tired of watching movies on my laptop and reading books. Plus, I knew I was putting a serious cramp in my sister's love life, and, given my reputation as a sex therapist, I didn't want them to be stuck doing quiet missionary position up in their bedroom as they tried not to disturb me.

But leaning against my front door and trying to summon the energy to open it and walk inside, I kind of missed Cassie's fussing and her couch.

And I missed Eshu. He was a demon that apparently worked with Lucien down in hell or something. I wasn't really sure what his position was, except that he was in and out of Cassie's house meeting with Lucien several times a day. He annoyed the heck out of Lucien, which I thought was funny. He also told the most horrible jokes, which I also thought was funny. The guy made my convalescence more than bearable, and I missed his silliness. I missed how he made faces at Lucien behind his back, how he deliberately annoyed a demon who was the son of Satan and evidently a big wig in hell. Eshu was a rebel, a joker, a contrarian. He took nothing seriously, made fun of everything, and did it all with a conspiratorial wink my way that made me feel like we were about to run away together and pull off a caper.

I missed Eshu. But I wasn't going to be that needy witch moping around my sister's house, trying to catch a glimpse of the demon. I was sure he was just as funny and charming with everyone he met. There was no need to read anything into his flirting and joking and embarrass myself by asking after him. Besides, I wasn't in any sort of condition to be dating right now. I'd died. I was still healing. My magic was on the fritz, although I hadn't told anyone about that little fact. I could barely walk from my office to my home.

Pulling myself straight, I managed to get my key in the lock, open the door, and stagger inside. There on my foyer table was a jug filled with green liquid and an index card with the words "drink me" looped around the top.

Glenda. I smiled, even though I knew the contents of this jug would be completely vile. With a shaking hand, I popped off the top and gulped down a few swallows, managing not to promptly throw it back up on my floor.

It tasted like latex paint and dog crap with some cotton fuzz for texture. But the moment it hit my stomach, I felt a surge of energy. Glenda's healing elixirs always worked their magic, even if they tasted horrible. The high of the potion had settled out by the time I'd walked to the kitchen and stuck the jug in a cabinet, leaving me feeling not like a super-hero but at least somewhat normal.

Normal enough to go over to Pistol Pete's and hang out?

It was Thursday night, and I hated to spend another evening in my pajamas on the couch, but I really didn't want to push it too far and end up a couple of miles from my house, ready to pass out. I glanced in my near-empty fridge and realized I'd need to go out tonight anyway to grocery shop. Hanging out at a bar my first day back would probably be pushing things a bit. Maybe tomorrow, when a band would be there. Yeah. If I felt good enough tomorrow after work, then maybe I'd get a burger at Pete's and hear the first set or two of the band.

I didn't bother taking a shower or freshening up my makeup, but I did change out of my pants suit and put my long hair up into a ponytail. Just as I was filling out my grocery list, there was a knock on my door. It opened to reveal two of my sisters. Cassie was carrying three plastic grocery bags, and Glenda was right behind her with an additional two.

Yes, all my sisters have a key to my house. My cousin Aaron as well. It's not like Cassie couldn't open my door with a wave of her hand and a quick incantation, and it made sense that the rest of my family could drop things off or pick things up without having to track me down for a key. My office I locked up like the treasure room in a castle, but my house didn't hold anything valuable or anything so personal that I didn't want my family to see. Plus, they were all terrified to snoop, convinced they'd find drawers full of sex toys and a blow-up doll in my bedroom.

They weren't wrong. About the sex toys, that is, not the blow--up doll. Although my "wild" sex toys only consisted of two vibrators, an anal plug, some lube, and a pair of nipple clamps that I'd quickly decided weren't for me.

"Haloooo!" Cassie cheerfully called. "How did your first day back go?"

I glanced over at Glenda, who put her finger to her lips and winked.

"Wonderful. I feel great." I totally didn't mention that I'd felt like dog crap until I'd drank Glenda's smoothie. Cassie worried enough about me as it was. And I appreciated that Glenda was willing to hide her assistance and make it seem as if I were completely recovered, otherwise I was sure Cassie would have bundled me up, stuffed me in her car, and had me back on her sofa for another week or two.

Cassie gave me a thorough looking-over as she put the grocery bags on the counter and began to unpack them. "You sure?"

"I'm sure." I grabbed the block of cheese and carton of milk and put them in the fridge while Glenda pulled two pounds of hamburger, a frozen pizza, and a box of donuts from her bags.

"Well, we figured you probably didn't have anything in your fridge that wasn't totally spoiled, and that you might be too tired to do any grocery shopping…" Cassie's voice trailed off and she made a hurt-sniff sort of noise. I hid a smile, knowing that my eldest sister needed to be needed.

"I really appreciate it," I told her. "I was just making a shopping list, but honestly I *am* kind of beat after not doing much for the last two weeks."

Cassie beamed. "Well, now you don't have to buy groceries. Or dinner. Look—Glenda and I brought some pork fried rice, wonton soup, and egg rolls. I thought we could all have dinner together."

I glanced over at my younger sister, who had pulled another jug of smoothie from her huge purse and was discretely shoving it into my cupboard. "I'd love that. Let me grab some plates and chopsticks."

"Oh, no you don't." Cassie took me by the shoulders and

steered me over to the couch. "Sit. Glenda and I have got this. You rest."

I sat and watched as my eldest sister took charge of everything, just like she always did. Some people might find Cassie bossy and overbearing, and I'll admit we sisters did sometimes chafe under her occasionally smothering care, but we loved her for it. She'd not hesitated to raise us all when our mother had hit the road, and that was saying a lot since she'd only been thirteen at the time. Plus, there were times when it was nice to be pampered and coddled. Actually, there were a lot of times when it was nice to be pampered and coddled.

Glenda walked over and handed me a bowl of wonton soup. "You doing okay?" she murmured. "Your aura looks a bit dim and colorless."

"My aura is a whole lot less dim and colorless thanks to your potion," I whispered back. "Without it, you guys would have come in to me passed out on the floor."

Glenda grimaced, shooting Cassie a quick glance. "Glad that didn't happen. Cassie would have hauled you back to her house and tied you to the sofa."

"Don't I know it." I let out an exasperated huff. "I just want to get my life back, you know? I want to get back to my clients, back to my hobbies, back to my routine."

Glenda reached down to give me a quick hug. "I know. Just don't push things too fast. You almost died. Take all the time you need."

I *had* died. And going through that made me a bit frantic about taking advantage of the time I had. I didn't want to spend another two weeks on Cassie's sofa—two weeks I'd never get back. I might die next week or next month or next year, and I wanted to spend every moment I had left doing the things I loved and not "taking it easy". There was nothing like an actual death experience to make a witch cherish the little things in life and knowingly live in the moment.

Cassie came over with plates of fried rice and egg rolls, plus a handful of chopsticks. She and Glenda joined me on the sofa, and we all ate, talking about our jobs and discussing whether we should have meatloaf or pot roast for this Sunday's family dinner.

"How are things with Lucien?" I asked Cassie. "He seemed a bit upset about something going on in the third circle of hell yesterday."

A bit upset was a massive understatement. I'd thought for a moment there he was going to burn down Cassie's house. Or possibly set Eshu on fire. I got the idea the whole blame-the-messenger thing was big among demons.

Cassie rolled her eyes and took a second to swallow her mouthful of fried rice. "It's not good. He might have to go down there for a few days and straighten things out."

Glenda grimaced. "What happened?"

"Evidently some communications got mixed up and a few demons got pissed at each other and it all escalated." Cassie waved an eggroll for emphasis. "He's blaming Eshu for screwing something up."

I felt a bit indignant about that. "Don't make poor Eshu the scapegoat. It's not like demons aren't ready to throw down over the stupidest thing. Remember last Sunday when Lucien nearly beheaded Hadur over sun dried tomatoes in the salad?"

"I'm with Hadur on that one," Glenda chimed in. "Sun dried tomatoes are an absolutely delicious addition to both salads *and* wood-fired pizza."

"Lucien can't do nightshade stuff," Cassie explained. "And dried makes it worse. Last time he ate tomatoes, he had to sleep in the guest room. His gas was bad enough to kill an army of goblins with one noxious shot."

I shuddered. "Well, he didn't have to eat the salad. There was no need to get up in Hadur's face about it."

"Lucien needs his greens. He has to have a diet with lots of fiber," Cassie shot back, defending her demon. "Hadur did it on purpose and didn't tell him until he'd already eaten half the salad. We missed out on sex that night because I didn't want to have to screw while wearing a gas mask."

Glenda slapped her hands over her ears. "Don't want to hear this."

I, on the other hand, totally wanted to hear it. Patting Cassie on the knee, I sent her a sympathetic look. "Sexual relations are a key component to your and Lucien's relationship. That must have been difficult for the both of you."

"It was." Cassie pouted. "And it was my turn to be on top, too."

"Not listening," Glenda announced.

"Perhaps you can double up this Sunday to make up for it?" I suggested. "You be on top for morning sex, and he can do doggy-style, or get a blow job, or spend some time going down on you after dinner."

Cassie's eyes got a faraway look. "Oh…. yes. That would be amazing. All of those. Lucien has remarkable stamina, and it only takes him a few minutes to recover. I wish I bounced back that quick."

"So…how about the weather?" Glenda chimed in. "Think we'll get some rain this week? It's a bit dry this summer, and we could really use a good shower."

I held back giving them some tips on shower sex and how golden showers between consenting adults were a perfectly acceptable kink in spite of public opinion and took pity on my sister. Glenda wasn't at all a prude, but she wasn't into what she called "oversharing."

"I just hope the rain holds off a bit longer," I told her. "I've been cooped up for two weeks on Cassie's couch and really want to soak up a bit of sun."

"Speaking of my couch, did you know that crazy Eshu calls you 'couch-witch'?" Cassie laughed. "We've told him your name a dozen times. It's like he can't remember it, although Lucien says he does that sort of thing on purpose to be annoying."

I took a bite of my eggroll, trying to keep my expression bland. Inside I was blushing and flustered because I thought it was cute. Couch-witch. He was so funny.

"He drove Lucien nuts asking where you were," Cassie continued. "The guy wasn't paying one bit of attention to what he was supposed to. Instead he was looking under the couch and in the closets, wanting to know where you lived."

"He was?" I tried really hard to keep the bubbly joy out of my voice.

"He's such an idiot." Cassie rolled her eyes. "Of course we didn't tell him. What a fool. Drives Lucien nuts. I think he'd ban him from the house if he didn't need him. He's the only demon who's allowed in heaven."

The bubbly joy vanished. Eshu *wasn't* an idiot. Yes, he was a clown, a funny guy, but that didn't make him stupid. Not that it mattered. I'd probably never see him again. He'd forget about me by tomorrow, and it's not like he ever came by Cassie's house when we were all there. I never would have met him if I hadn't been convalescing on her couch for two weeks.

Couch-witch. That was so stinking cute.

"Enough about Lucien. How are things with the were-wolves?" Glenda asked.

"Tense." Cassie shoved the last bit of eggroll in her mouth and picked up her soup. "Sadly, Dallas' mating ceremony didn't hold off tensions for long. There have been raids on both sides and some vandalism of the road going up to the compound."

"I would have thought Dallas would be too busy locked in a bedroom on his honeymoon to be fighting," I commented.

"Me, too." Glenda took a bite of her egg roll. "The way that werewolf acts, you'd think sex was his number one priority. I had to threaten to poison his well with a limp-dick potion to make him stop grabbing my ass."

"I think the honeymoon would have given us a few months of cease-fire if Clinton hadn't taken advantage of the wedding and made a move," Cassie said. "I really don't know the exact details of what's been happening so far, but I know it involves a lot of peeing to move territory markers, as well as attacking scouts during the night and roughing them up. Oh, and Clinton's guys bombed out a section of the road. Make sure you use four-wheel drive if you need to go up to the compound because they dug the crap out of the road. Potholes and ditches all over the place."

I grimaced. "And of course Dallas retaliated."

Cassie rolled her eyes. "Werewolf egos. Of course he retaliated. He's not going to let his pack think he's weak by letting that sort of thing go. I really don't know what to do at this point. I've gotten in Dallas's face, burned the beard off Clinton's face, threatened the pair of them. Neither one is going to back down."

"Just blow up the mountain and be done with it. No more werewolves, and it would shave twenty minutes off the commute time to Fairview."

I choked back a laugh because Glenda was kidding. At least, I thought she was kidding. Cassie was the only one of us with an explosive temper, but Glenda had this dry pragmatic thing going on that made me sometimes wonder about her moral alignment.

"Trust me, I've considered it," Cassie said. "There aren't

many options left, honestly. I've put down my foot when it comes to some things, but I can't change hundreds of years of culture and tradition in a few months."

Thanks to Cassie, wolves were now allowed to leave the pack and live in Accident without being hunted down. But as my session with Alberta and Shelby had revealed, being a lone wolf wasn't all it was cracked up to be. Still, the option was there. And Cassie had told Dallas that werewolves would be held to the laws of Accident, regardless of what their own rules and regulations allowed for. Supposedly that meant due process for any werewolf violating pack law. Basically, they could keep their traditions and culture unless it went directly against the laws of Accident.

Of course, what happened up in the mountains didn't always come to light down here in the valley. And if it came to it, our legal system didn't really have the power to enforce law in a pack of hundreds of werewolves. At least not without seven witches backing them up.

But that would be a solution of might, and I wasn't the only one who knew violence wasn't the long-term solution to what we'd come to jokingly call the Werewolf Problem. Bending them to our will by force would only get us temporary, grudging compliance that would rebound and smack us in the asses the moment our backs were turned.

"So, you're just going to let them go at it and hope for the best?" Glenda asked.

Cassie shrugged. "I can yell and set fire to shit all I want, but I can't stop a werewolf war. I've told both Dallas and Clinton this can't affect anyone outside the two packs, and no fighting can take place off the mountain. I also let them know that any werewolf who wants refuge from the fighting is welcome in town, and I won't tolerate that being held against them when the dust settles."

Glenda snorted. "Yeah. Good luck with that. I'm not

Ophelia but let me give you my prediction right here: Clinton and his pack are killed. Dallas loses twenty or so of his pack in the fighting. Half the mountain is torn up and all their crops and livestock destroyed. Refugees will be exiled, and we'll have to take up collections to feed the remaining werewolves through the winter or watch them starve."

It was a sobering prediction, but neither Cassie nor I denied its validity.

"Dallas won't budge at all?" I asked.

"Nope. He's exiled Clinton and the werewolves that left with him and says they need to get off the mountain. I at least got him to say he'd allow them all to remain in Accident as lone wolves, but he won't make any promises on whether the individuals in his pack won't continue to attack them or not. It's too personal for most of the pack, he says."

"Would Clinton be open to that?" I asked, knowing the answer.

"Not a chance. He wants part of the mountain, and he's not leaving."

It bothered me that there wasn't some peaceful solution to all this. I got why Clinton had formed a splinter pack. He'd chafed under his father's rule and knew there were other members of the pack that felt the same. The werewolf answer to that was to challenge the alpha, but Clinton knew who would win that fight, and it would have been a fight to the death.

It was a huge mountain. There was no reason beyond pride that Dallas couldn't allow his only son to establish a sub-pack on a section of neighboring land. Maybe there was some avenue to peace that hadn't yet been explored. Maybe there was some sort of compromise that would work for both of them. I didn't know what that was, and it was clear none of my sisters did, either.

"Oh, and this all reminds me," Cassie added. "Do you

think you could pull together a charm or two for me? In the next week or two? I've got a case on the other side of the wards and it wouldn't be good if the humans discovered the defendant was a yeti. I just need to improve the odds that the judge will agree to a change of venue so the trial can be held here in Accident."

I sucked in a breath and looked down at my soup, appetite completely gone. "Sure. No problem."

It *was* a problem. I just didn't want Cassie or any of my sisters to know it was a problem.

We finished our dinner and my sisters did a quick clean up before leaving. Once they were gone, I pulled my magical supplies out of the closet and spread them out on my coffee table.

A luck charm or two. That used to be so easy. But now…. It wasn't as if my magic was *totally* gone. I could still feel a tiny thread of it whispering through my body, but when I went to do anything magical, nothing happened. It was as if I called, and either the magic that remained was too faint to do any good or just didn't respond at all.

Part of me feared this was the way it would always be. Part of me feared my magic would return, but that it would be…wonky. Maybe charms wouldn't turn out like they were supposed to. Maybe they'd end up being hexes or not providing the type of luck I intended—which really wasn't a big deal when all I was trying to do was make sure there was enough hot water for my shower, or that there was a front parking space at the mall. A potential for exposure of our world though…that was big. I didn't want to screw that up.

I hoped that I just needed a little longer to heal and then everything would be back to normal. As for Cassie's request, well, I had another week or so to rest up, to drink Glenda's disgusting potions, and to get my strength back. I'd wait on these charms and maybe try them next week. I was sure by then that I'd be fully recovered and would have no problem imbuing them with the appropriate magic.

Yep, I told myself, *I'll be fine by next week*. That's when I'll do these charms. By next week, everything is going to be back to normal.

CHAPTER 3

ESHU

I knocked on the door, hoping that this was the correct house. I'd been to six so far this evening and had all sorts of creatures spit at me, try to stab me with tridents, and curse me in a weird fae language. I guess some folk don't like to be woken up at two in the morning by a demon at their door demanding to know if his couch-witch resided therein.

No one answered at this house, so I knocked again with more force, then tried to peek through a side window, nearly falling over the porch rail and into a prickly bush with fragrant white flowers. A light came on, and I readied myself for spit, or knives, or whatever.

Instead, the door opened and there stood my beloved, her hair a sable mess of tangled waves, her blue eyes full of sleep. There was a deep crease on her cheek, probably from her pillow, and her left boob looked as if it were about ready to escape from her tank top.

I stared at the left boob, willing it to fly free, then looked down to her pink lacy underwear and naked legs. They were tanned and strong, with broad thighs and muscled calves. I couldn't help but imagine them wrapped around my waist.

"Eshu." Her voice was burred with sleep and I felt myself grow hard at the sound of it.

"My couch-witch. I've found you." I pushed past her and looked around. It was a nice home. Warm. Comfortable. Lots of color.

"What are you doing here?"

She sounded confused, but not displeased. I looked down and aside from staring at the rebellious boob, I noted the shadows under her eyes that I hadn't seen previously.

I know. I'm a bad potential lover for not having noticed, but in my defense, her boob was *almost* out of her tank top.

"I'm here to see *you*, my couch-witch. But why are you not on the couch sleeping? You look exhausted."

She ran a hand through her hair, making parts of it stick up here and there. "Because I had to answer the door, you dork. And I don't normally sleep on—"

The rest of her sentence was cut off with a squeal because I'd picked her up and began walking over to the couch. Staggering actually, because she was a bit heavier than I'd thought. Thankfully, I didn't drop her because I was pretty sure I'd never be able to get any sexy witch action if I dumped my beloved onto the floor.

"Here." I plopped her down on the couch, saddened that the motion hadn't freed the nearly escaped boob. Then I went into her kitchen and looked in her fridge. "Why don't you have any grapes? You need to have grapes."

"I haven't been to the grocery store, and I don't normally eat grapes. I think Cassie brought some blueberries, though." Her voice was husky/sleepy. It made me wonder once more if the time was right to show her my enormous love-lance or if more wooing was in order.

I grabbed the blueberries and sat on the coffee table

beside the couch, looking around for a fan. What was the problem with this witch that she didn't have a fan, nor grapes? How was I supposed to show her my adoration if I couldn't fan her and feed her grapes?

Needing to improvise, I grabbed a pillow off the couch and tried to fan her with it, accidently bopping her on the head.

"Hey! What are you—"

I shoved a few blueberries in her mouth then began to recite the naughty limerick I'd composed in her honor. Every time she went to say something, I fed her more blueberries, and fanned with increasing vigor.

I decided to stop with the blueberries when she began to laugh and nearly choked on them.

"Stop! Eshu, cut it out. I'm not hungry, and I don't want to have a pillow fight right now, if that's what you're trying to do. I'm tired. I had a really exhausting day, and I need to sleep."

I set the pillow and the blueberries aside, pouting a bit as she adjusted the tank top and secured the renegade boob in place.

"I'm sorry." She reached out and touched my thigh. I silently willed her fingers to go higher, but to no avail. "I'm so happy to see you. I'm glad you came over here, really, I am. But it's late and I'm so tired. Maybe we can take a raincheck? You can shove fruit down my throat and whack me with a pillow while reciting bawdy poetry another night?"

I'd rather shove something else down her throat, but clearly that wasn't going to happen tonight. Instead I scooted her legs over, sat down on the couch, then repositioned her legs on top of my lap. "Why are you so tired, my couch-witch? I assumed your reclining state was so that the other mortals could worship you accordingly. I never thought that it was because you needed extra rest."

"The accident," she murmured in that sleepy voice that went right to my groin. "I was recovering on Cassie's couch, and I thought I was okay, but I guess not. I'm so tired."

I ran my hands up her bare legs, a thrill racing through me at the soft *mmm* noise she made. "I know you told me you'd had an accident, but I hadn't realized it was so serious."

"I went to the hospital and was on a couch for two weeks." She chuckled. "What did you think, I stubbed my toe or something?"

"A hangnail? A papercut? A bad case of split ends?"

"Brat." She smacked me with the pillow, then lay back with a contented sigh as I kept caressing her legs.

"Two weeks is plenty of rest," I told her. "You should be good as new by now."

She sighed. "I'm not. Cassie wants me to go back on her couch so she can fuss over me, but I wanted to get back to my life. Outside of your visits, all I was doing was lying there, streaming Netflix, and obsessing about…things. But I'm not doing good. I'm so tired. Glenda's smoothies are the only thing keeping me going. And…mmm, that feels good."

I kept doing the thing that felt good and she relaxed into my touch, turning her face to the pillow and closing her eyes. There was something beyond her easily depleted physical energy that was worrying her—something about her town, her responsibilities, her magic. But I could tell she didn't want to talk about it right now. I could tell she didn't want to even think about it.

It scared her. Something worried and scared her, and I didn't want my couch-witch to be afraid. I wanted her to laugh. And to make those happy contented noises she was making.

Well, *had* been making. Right now, she wasn't making those noises anymore; she was snoring.

I looked down at her face, wanting to kiss her. But fairy

tales to the contrary, I knew from experience that often did not go well. Kissing a sleeping person whom one had been in the happy habit of kissing while awake was fine. But a first kiss while they were asleep? There was a good sixty percent chance that was going to result in a fist to the face and not amazing sex.

So gave her legs one last caress, got up, put a blanket over her, then left before I decided it was worth the risk of get punched in the face.

CHAPTER 4

SYLVIE

The next morning, I chugged down a glass full of Glenda's smoothie concoction, hoping it would be enough to get me through the day. Then I chased it with strong black coffee in an effort to get the foul taste out of my mouth. My first appointment was at ten, so I had time to scramble a few eggs and actually have a decent breakfast.

I felt...better. Maybe it was a good night's sleep in my own home, although my couch wasn't anywhere near as comfortable as my bed. Either way, I'd slept soundly all night, barely moving an inch. I woke up refreshed and happy.

Eshu had come over late at night. I was sure of that, even though it felt like a dream. He'd obviously slipped out sometime before I woke, but I distinctly remembered dragging myself out of bed to answer the door, having him try to cram blueberries in my mouth, and whack me with a pillow. Then he'd done this incredibly erotic leg massage that had made me wish I hadn't been so tired.

Would he be back? He'd clearly gone to a lot of effort to track me down because I was sure none of my sisters told him where I lived. But Eshu was...well, Eshu. I wasn't sure if his interest would last more than a day or two, if even that. I might not see him for months only to have him show up at my door again as if he'd never left.

I knew better than to try to change a guy like that or to expect anything more than who he was. I only hoped the next time he came around, I was more awake and could take that leg massage to the intended conclusion.

I couldn't get too attached to him, though. I was vulnerable and recovering from a life-changing event. Could I enjoy what I needed, but not expect anything more, or would I end up with a bruised heart after he'd moved on to the next woman?

But I couldn't obsess about that right now. It was Friday, and even though I'd only been back to my life and work for two days, I was thrilled. Maybe I'd head to Pistol Pete's for the band tonight. Then Saturday I'd have breakfast at the diner, run a few errands, take an afternoon nap, and get ready for The Game.

The Game. I'd been on couch-rest for two weeks and left my adventuring party about to enter a condemned building in their perilous quest for the Stone of Power. There would be aliens. There would be monsters. There most definitely wouldn't be the Stone in the treasure chest they were so determined to open. Some of them might die and have to roll up new characters, but we'd all enjoy ourselves for four or five hours while eating pizza and drinking beer.

It felt so good to get back to normal, to the life I'd had before I'd died. But as I thought of my weekend plans, my mind drifted back to a certain demon—one who'd made me laugh those two weeks on the couch. Would he stop by tonight? Next week? Next month?

If not, perhaps I could come up with a lame reason to go hang out at Cassie's house with Lucien one day this week, just to see if he'd show up. Or I could just be honest with myself and ask Cassie about him.

No. I'd gone through enough. I didn't need to be chasing after some demon that I was pretty sure was a total playboy. If he stopped by, I'd indulge in whatever he offered. And then I'd try hard to forget about him just as quickly as he forgot about me.

Brushing Eshu once more out of my mind, I stacked the dishes in the sink, gathered up a sweater and my purse, and headed to the office.

My first client of the day was Henriette, who was one of my life-coach clients. After a lifetime of same old-same old, she was trying to discover who she truly was inside. It was sort of a banshee mid-life crisis. Henriette's current goal was to find something new and rewarding to focus on in the second half of her very long life, to find a passion hobby.

The past month I'd had her write down all the things she'd always found intriguing but never done. Narrowing them down, we ended up with a list of five. Her goal was to try one item from that list each week, then be prepared to discuss the experience at our meeting.

Sky diving. Knife-throwing. Irish dance. White water rafting. Plein air painting.

Yep, plein air painting. That's what Henriette had spent the last three weeks working on because we hadn't had a meeting due to my accident and recuperation and she wasn't the sort of banshee who would proceed onto the next item on the list without my approval and guidance.

So far, we'd explored Irish dance, which the banshee had thoroughly enjoyed and had been actually quite good at, and knife throwing. She wasn't as good at knife throwing, and after an unannounced demonstration in our session, I'd done what all my training forbade me to do and informed her she should give that one up immediately.

Let's just say I'm glad I'm a luck witch because I'm pretty sure otherwise I would have spent some time in the hospital recovering from knife wounds.

Henriette was waiting for me outside my office door. One thing about banshees—they're prompt. I guess it was that whole harbinger of death thing. It made me wonder if there was some connection between them and reapers. I'd have to ask Nash some time if he ever worked with banshees or if they'd been handled by some different department or his soul-reaping organization, whatever it was. I'd asked Henriette once about her banshee nature, and she'd told me it wasn't like a job where she had to run around and shriek before every person in the world died. She said it was more like an impulse that hit her, and she never knew exactly who her wailing was for. She could be in a crowded shopping mall and bam—ear-splitting screaming. Moving to Accident made life much easier on her and her sisters. A town full of supernaturals meant there weren't a lot of deaths to herald. And here there was no fear that someone would call mall security and haul her off for a psychiatric evaluation.

I let Henriette in and noticed that she was carrying what appeared to be the world's largest briefcase. Once we were in my office, she unzipped it and I realized it was, in fact, the world's largest art portfolio case.

It seemed the banshee had taken her plein air assignment seriously. I watched as she unpacked and displayed the various artwork, her black hair a lovely complement to her dark-gray skin. Had she colored it? It seemed shinier and a deeper shade than it was when we last met. And she'd coiled it up into a clip, the tail sticking up in a spray of ebony locks.

Hair color or not, Henriette seemed to be livelier, more animated than she'd been when she first started coming to me. It was a good sign—one that made me think we were on the right track here.

"What do you think?" She stood back and expanded her arms as if she were on a game show modeling the prizes.

"Henriette, it's what *you* think that matters. These projects are all about you finding what activities bring you joy. It's the journey that matters, not the destination."

"Yes, but are these the sort of destinations you'd not be ashamed to hang on your wall? Things you might actually praise or even pay for?"

I eyed them closely. They were amateurish in my estimation, but I was no art critic. One was a nymph sitting by a stream, combing her hair. Another showed a cow grazing in a field. Another was a scene from our own Main Street with the diner in the corner and John the Cyclops' car parked out front.

"I like them. They're not my style, and I don't think they'd be sellable as art, but I believe you could hang them on your wall and not be ashamed to show them to your friends and family."

She nodded, eyeing the paintings with renewed interest.

"But the real question," I continued, "is did you enjoy painting them? Let's talk about your mental and emotional state as you were creating each of these."

"Meditative," she immediately offered. "I didn't worry about whether I was doing it right or if the end result was going to be a piece of crap or not. I just let myself fall into the mixing of paints and making a scene come to life on the canvas."

I nodded. The Irish dancing had made her feel alive and powerful. It had been exhilarating, and she'd taken pride in mastering the sometimes-complicated steps. Knife throwing had been cathartic, but while I'm all for catharsis, the potential for town casualties was considerable. Painting seemed like it might be a beneficial thing for Henriette to continue pursuing.

"Is this the sort of activity you might enjoy doing weekly or monthly?" I asked. "When life gets stressful, it's nice to be able to turn to something that calms you, that centers you."

"I think weekly," she replied after some thought.

"Like the Irish dancing, the important thing is the way the activity makes you feel. If you find something else that has the same result, feel free to switch or even add the other activity into your schedule."

"Like pottery, or fiber arts." She pursed her lips and nodded. "I was thinking the same thing about skydiving. It's probably going to give me the same feelings as the Irish dancing, although maybe more of a rush because it's dangerous. If I like that, then I could do Irish dancing every other week, and maybe skydiving every few months or a couple times in the summer."

"Exactly. And the same with white water rafting. You may end up spacing out those three activities or alternating between them depending on exactly what you feel like doing."

"The knife throwing was fun," she added with a sideways grin. "Maybe I'll try that again."

"I suggest you stick to dancing, and possibly skydiving or white water rafting. The knife throwing was going to get someone killed. As in, me or possibly one of the humans in town. At the very best, you were going to impale a werewolf and find yourself eviscerated in response."

She laughed. "You're right, especially about the werewolves. They don't take stabbing lightly. Ask me how I know."

I couldn't resist that. "Okay. How do you know?"

Banshees were gossips, and Henriette and her two sisters were the most gossipy gossips I'd ever known.

"Chantal said that Kirk said that Ellen said that yesterday night at Petunia's Bait, Auto Repair, and Beer, Bart Dickskin got stabbed and next thing you know, there's car parts and buckets of worms flying and people smashing bottles of Budweiser over each other's heads. Sheriff Oakes got called out, but by the time he got there, everyone had scattered."

I stared at her. "Wait…what? Who stabbed Bart? And why? What happened?"

Petunia's was normally a pretty chill place, with residents hanging out to wait while their cars were repaired or discussing fishing before picking up bait and beer. The owner normally didn't tolerate any sort of fighting or arguments. Petunia was a boar-shifter. And a guy. I've got no idea why he was called Petunia, but no one made fun of the name, just like no one made fun of the Dickskin werewolves' name. Well, at least not to their face.

She sighed, clearly thinking I was an idiot for my inability to follow the convoluted story. "Melvin was there, chewing the fat and getting some work done on a carburetor, and Bart came in to pick up bait and beer. They know they're supposed to be civil when they're in town, but you know werewolves aren't real good at being civil."

The light of understanding went on in my head. "So, Melvin is one of Dallas's…cousins? Nephews? And Bart is part of Clinton's pack?"

She sent me a scathing glance. "They're both Dickskins—third cousins twice removed of Dallas. Melvin is with Clinton's group, and Bart is part of Dallas's group. Goodness sakes, Sylvie. You're a Perkins; you're supposed to know these things."

She was right, but the werewolves had never been so involved in town activities and affairs that I'd learned all of their names. Nor was I positive who was with what faction.

"So, I get that there was some tension between Bart and Melvin, but why the stabbing?"

She shrugged. "Werewolves get stabby. It happens."

"But was there an argument?" I pressed. She was a banshee. They knew everything that happened in this town. "Why didn't Petunia throw them all out?"

"Of course there was an argument. And Petunia wasn't there. He was out getting an engine part from the Chevy dealer outside the wards. First there was some name calling. Then there were some not-so-subtle digs at bathroom habits and hunting abilities. Then Bart 'accidently' threw an elbow when walking by Melvin to supposedly get a six pack of beer from the walk-in. Melvin spun around with a screwdriver in his hand and jabbed it into Bart's thigh. All completely an accident, of course."

Of course. I could only imagine the sort of force Melvin would have needed to use to actually stab a screwdriver into someone's leg. None of this was an accident, and it was absolutely typical of what happened when werewolves were either drinking or pissed off about something.

Stuff like this made me wish they'd all pack up and move somewhere other than Accident.

"Bart yelped when he got stabbed with the screwdriver, and things started flying. Took about five seconds before everyone else had joined in and there were broken beer bottles and worms all over the place. Petunia had an absolute shit-fit when he got back and saw the place."

I'll bet. "And they were both gone by the time the sheriff got there." I repeated her earlier statement.

"Yep." She rolled her eyes. "I kinda wish those werewolves would just go to war and get it over with. Least that way they'd keep it up on the mountain and stop fighting with each other in town. Every time one of Dallas's wolves and one of Clinton's wolves end up in the same place, fur flies."

I thought about the issues with the werewolves while Henriette and I discussed her skydiving trip next week and how joining a book club could expand both her social activities and give her an opportunity to expand her reading interests.

She left and I prepared for my next and final client of the day, wondering if Henriette was right. If things up on Heartbreak Mountain came to a head, and the werewolves went to war, would it be for the best? Would a brief war allow us to settle into the sort of peace we'd had before?

The loss of lives wouldn't be worth less fighting in town, though. Something needed to happen to bring about peace. I just didn't see violence as the solution.

But what was the solution?

My next client was a werewolf, but not one I could ask about the situation on the mountain, at least not about current happenings. Stanley had been a spy for Clinton, remaining in Dallas's compound. He'd been aware of the sabotage of Bronwyn's truck and Clinton's efforts to pin that whole mess on Dallas. He'd gone to Bronwyn and Hadur and let them know what was happening, thus betraying both the werewolf packs on the mountain. Dallas and Clinton would have killed him for that, but he'd become a lone wolf, living in town under our protection and completely ostracized by both packs, just like Shelby.

Unlike Shelby, he didn't have someone he loved to help ease the loss of everything he'd ever known in his life. Stanley was lonely, depressed, and I worried he might do something drastic. I was glad when he'd taken me up on my offer of therapy, and I breathed a sigh of relief every time he showed up to one of our appointments.

The door chimed, and Stanley walked in, clutching the amulet that allowed him to come and go from my office undetected. He was seventyish, which made him middle-aged for a werewolf. He *looked* like a forty-year-old construction worker with his dusty jeans, worn t-shirt, and leathery tanned skin. There were lines in the corners of his eyes from squinting, and a thick scar ran from his left cheekbone to the corner of his mouth. Werewolves had amazing healing. I didn't want to contemplate how terrible that injury must have been to have left a scar.

Stanley held out a hand to shake mine. His fingers were clean and calloused, with black-stained cuticles. Petunia had hired him to help with his auto-repair business and seeing the stained fingers gave me hope that Stanley would find some comfort and happiness in his new job.

"Hoping you weren't at work when things went down the other day at Petunia's between Melvin and Bart," I commented.

A sad expression flickered across his face before he twisted his lips in an ironic smile. "Yeah, I was there. Just kept out of the way. It's not like Melvin or Bart were going to talk to me or even acknowledge my existence. When a werewolf comes in to pick up bait and beer or to get his truck fixed, someone else always needs to help them. They won't even look me in the face."

A mixture of sorrow and fury stirred in my chest. This bullshit totally had to stop. It wasn't just the two packs ready to kill each other off. It wasn't just the werewolves coming into town and starting fights. It wasn't just their taking justice into their own hands. Stanley had done the right thing and in doing so, he'd lost everything. That was so unfair. But what could I do about it? I couldn't force werewolves to be nice to Stanley.

"Sit." I gestured to the comfy, pillow-strewn client chairs. "Tea? Or coffee?"

Stanley sat and gave me a sheepish grin. "Tea, please. Do you have that berry blend herbal?"

I smiled and handed him a wooden box with all my teas, then poured him a steaming mug of water from the kettle. Setting it down on the table beside him, I took a seat.

"How are things?" I grimaced. "I'm so sorry I had to cancel the last two weeks."

He plopped his tea bag into the mug and smiled. "I heard. Glad you're okay, Sylvie. Getting electrocuted is no fun. Good thing you're a luck witch or you might not be here now."

I shivered, then tried to push the fears and memories into the back corner of my mind. "Yes, I was very lucky. So...last time we met, our goals were around work, making your house a home, and finding some potential non-werewolf friends. Let's talk about work first."

"I like working for Petunia. He's a shifter, so he gets me in a way lots of other people in town don't. He's got some of the same issues since he's the only boar shifter in town. I like working with my hands. I've always enjoyed fixing things. Money's good and Petunia's a fair boss."

I smiled. "That's great, Stanley! I believe that having fulfilling work is so important to personal happiness. Do you think you're feeling better now that you've got a job and you're liking the work and the environment?"

He nodded. "Days off and evenings are tough, though. When I'm at work, I'm busy and happy, but as soon as I go home, it all feels like a load of rocks crashing down on my head."

"Then let's talk about making your house a home."

The hour went fast, and in the end, I had a horrible feeling that Stanley might not make it. He had a job he loved, but couldn't seem to connect with anyone in town, and his depression hit hard every night when he got home. He hadn't shifted into his wolf form in three weeks, hadn't hunted in four weeks. He brushed off my suggestions of connecting with Shelby, saying they hadn't been friendly before and he couldn't see how getting together with her would help at all.

Just before he left, Stanley turned to me and once more voiced his wish that he wasn't shunned.

"They don't have to accept me back into either pack," he said. "I just wish they'd nod to me on the street. I wish they'd talk to me, maybe join me for a beer or something now and then. I miss my kind. I think if I could just connect with one werewolf now and then, I'd be okay. It's the total isolation that's killing me, Sylvie."

I struggled to keep tears in check at his confession and reached out to touch his shoulder. "Was there someone in the pack you were particularly close to? A best friend? A potential mate you were wooing?"

He laughed. "No potential mate. But Bart and I were good friends."

I blinked. "Bart Dickskin? The same Bart Dickskin that got stabbed with a screwdriver at Petunia's the other day?"

He nodded. "Nothing hurt more than having him come in and act like I was a stranger. Not even a stranger. He acted like I wasn't even there. And when he got stabbed with that screwdriver and there was that huge fight, I went over to see if he was okay, and he didn't even look at me."

I swallowed hard, knowing how gutted I'd be if I'd been in this werewolf's situation. "Please hang in there, Stanley. You call me if you need to talk, okay? Enjoy work. Do the things we discussed. And we'll talk more next week."

He smiled and patted my hand, then turned to leave. I milled about my office, cleaning up the tea mugs, turning off the kettle, locking my papers away. It was just after noon. I was hungry and feeling the exhaustion I'd not been able to fully conquer since my accident. I needed to go home, eat a sandwich, drink Glenda's smoothie, and take a nap.

Instead, I walked home, got in my car, and drove up to Heartbreak Mountain.

CHAPTER 5

The werewolves were on high alert, following me up the mountain to the compound and announcing my arrival with barks and howls. I parked and exited my car to see half a dozen werewolves in human form and three in wolf form, all clustered around my vehicle and eyeing me uneasily.

"Relax," I told them. "I'm not here to burn anyone's beard off or anything. I just wanted to talk to Bart."

They all exchanged glances. "That fight at Petunia's wasn't his fault," an older female wolf told me. "Bart didn't start it. Melvin stabbed him with a screwdriver. He's the one you need to be arresting."

I held out my hands. "Do I look like I'm arresting anyone? I just want to talk to Bart."

They eyed me suspiciously. "What do ya need him for?" the older female finally asked.

Obviously, I couldn't tell them the real reason I wanted to speak to Bart. Luckily, I'd been secretly providing counseling sessions to werewolves for years, and I'd learned a lot about their culture. Basically, I knew what their weaknesses were, and I felt no regret at all about using them right now.

"He was one of the winners in the firehouse raffle."

I could practically feel the excitement running through the nine werewolves in front of me. One of the ones in wolf form licked his muzzle and did a four-legged happy dance.

"What did he win?" the older female squealed, clapping her hands together.

Werewolves weren't the only beings in Accident that adored games, but they especially liked ones where there was a prize to the winner. Didn't matter if it was a ball of yarn or a scrap of paper, they'd brag and show it off to everyone like they'd just won a dragon's hoard.

"I'm only telling Bart." That announcement ratcheted up the excitement considerably, and two of the four-legged werewolves raced off. I was sure they were going to find Bart.

"Was it the latch-hook rug with the birds on it?" the older woman asked. "The bread maker? The month's supply of gluten-free avocado toast?"

"I'll bet it was the free mani-pedi from Evaline's," a young male werewolf said, glancing at his fingernails longingly. "Lucky bastard."

"Or that pheasant from Dale's Taxidermy," another young male added. "I really wanted that."

The two werewolves in wolf form raced back, yipping and barking. The older female turned to them, then back to me. "Bart's in his den. He asked if you wouldn't mind visiting him there since he's still a little gimpy from getting stabbed yesterday."

Werewolves were very private about their homes. Outsiders were usually met at the main compound house, or…well, outside. Bart must have been really hurt to still be suffering from the injury enough not to hobble over to the main house.

"No problem." I followed the two wolf-form werewolves through a maze of alleyways. Other werewolves peeked out from windows and doorways with curiosity. A few of them followed me until one of my escorts turned and growled. Everyone scattered back to their houses, and we continued to the very edge of the row to a small one-story cabin.

At one of my escorts' scratching, a voice called to come in. I swung the door open and turned to the two wolves.

"No listening," I told them. "Let Bart be the one to tell everyone what he won. Don't spoil his surprise."

They both regarded me with huge brown eyes, then nodded and took off, trotting down the lane. I went in, closing the door behind me and letting my eyes adjust a bit to the dim lighting of Bart's home.

It was one big main room with a door that I was pretty sure led to the bathroom and another beside it that probably led to a small bedroom. The main room had a kitchenette off to the side with an island-bar type dining area. Two giant cushioned sofas took up most of the room. Bart lay on one, his leg bandaged around the thigh and propped up on a leather ottoman.

"What did I win?" His eyes glowed, the normal brown turning gold with his excitement.

I sat across from him. "Nothing. It was my excuse to get to see you."

I felt bad at the disappointment in his face. "Really? I was hoping it was that latch-hook rug with the birds on it."

"Better luck next time," I told him. "I actually wanted to talk to you about something else, and I need you to be absolutely honest with me."

He scowled. "It wasn't my fault. Melvin stabbed me with a screwdriver."

I rolled my eyes. "After you elbowed him. But I'm not here to talk to you about that. I'm here to discuss Stanley with you."

He eyed me uneasily. "Who? Don't know any Stanley."

I pulled a charm out of my pocket and set it on the table in front of us. It was a purple rabbit's foot with lines of glitter on the fur. I'd made a bunch of these early in the year because a witch who was a therapist never knew when she needed to talk to someone in private. The moment I walked in, I'd pinched the rabbit's foot to activate it. I figured it was a good time to put it in plain view and reassure Bart that just as no one holding one of my charms was seen coming or going from my office, no one lurking outside his cabin would have any idea what the heck we were talking about—even with super-duper werewolf hearing.

"He did the right thing, Bart. And because of that, he was faced with a choice of either being shunned or killed."

A muscle twitched in the werewolf's jaw. "He was spying on us for Clinton."

"And when he realized Clinton was trying to pin something on your pack that you all didn't do and when he realized my sister was caught in the middle and in danger, he stepped up. That's a hell of a lot more important to me than preferring one style of leadership over another."

"It's more than that. He's a traitor," Bart insisted.

"Because he felt it should be okay to have two packs on the mountain? That people should be able to want to live differently and not be exiled and shunned because of that?" I let that sink in for a moment. "You were his friend, Bart. You knew him better than probably anyone else in this pack. Is Stanley a traitor just because Dallas says so or because in your heart you know that to be so?"

He sighed. "I don't blame him; really, I don't. But let's face it, Dallas isn't going to let this thing with Clinton go. It's past the point of reconciliation, and it's embarrassing for him to have his own son snatch a section of territory and form his own pack. I picked my side, and now I gotta stick with it."

"I don't fault you for that, Bart. I'm still holding out hope that there can be a peaceful solution here, but I don't blame you at all for being loyal to your pack. I'm just asking you to consider other loyalties you might have."

He frowned. "What do you mean?"

"Stanley. He's having a hard time of it. I'm worried that he might think he made the wrong choice when he took exile over death."

Bart sat up in alarm, wincing and reaching out to grab his thigh with the motion. "I thought he was doing okay. I mean, I saw him there working at Petunia's on the cars. He was talking to a couple of mermen about something or another. Didn't look to me like he was regretting anything."

So, he *had* noticed his former friend, all while pretending to ignore him.

"Imagine having to live away from the werewolves you've spent your entire existence with. Imagine them not talking to you or even acknowledging your presence. Your friends. Your family. Nobody will even look at you. Shifting into wolf form just makes you feel more alone. You can't even hunt without missing your pack." I remembered something Shelby had said. "And at night during the full moon, you sit on your back porch and hear the howls up on the mountain and know that you'll never be a part of that again."

Bart swiped a quick hand under his eyes. "Can't do nothing about that, Sylvie. Dallas forbade us from having any contact with Stanley. Clinton did the same with his pack. If someone caught one of us talking to him or hunting with him, we'd be in big trouble. Maybe even find ourselves exiled as well if Dallas is in a bad mood."

"What if it wasn't forbidden? Would you see him then?"

He looked at me as if I were crazy. "Of course I would. He's my friend. I mean, he *was* my friend."

"So, you forgive him for spying on Dallas? For exposing Clinton's plans?"

Bart squirmed, looking down at his leg. "Him exposing Clinton's plans is what redeems him in my opinion. I still ain't happy about him spying on Dallas, but I get how people might want a different sort of leader. There's just things in place to address that."

"Challenges. Which are to the death."

"They're not always to the death," Bart protested. Then he met my gaze and lowered his eyes again. "Okay, most of the time they're to the death. But yeah. If someone wants a different alpha, that's what they do. It's the way it's always been."

"What if someone wants a different alpha but doesn't want to *be* that alpha? Doesn't the pack have some kind of say in the leader they get? Do you honestly feel the best leadership qualities are whoever can physically beat and kill anyone else in the pack?"

"It's tradition," he argued. "And no, it takes more than that. But when it comes down to it, the best at anything else in the world is gonna lose out to the strongest. That's why the strongest leads."

"And how long would the strongest lead if one hundred wolves all attacked him at once? Or just left? Let's say no one wants to have Dallas as an alpha, so they just left, like Clinton did with his pack. Is Dallas going to attack them with the ten or so wolves that remain? He can't be an alpha or even a force on this mountainside if no one follows him."

Bart sighed. "Look, Sylvie, I get where you're going with this, but me standing up against Dallas is only gonna get me killed. Clinton and his pack are probably all going to die in the next month or so anyway, and that will serve as a lesson to anyone who is thinking of doing what you're saying. Life here ain't bad. Dallas isn't a bad alpha. I don't have any problem with other people leaving. I don't have any problem with there being two or three packs, or people being lone wolves, or any of that. But I don't want to be the head on the chopping block if I go against what Dallas says."

"Someone needs to make a stand, Bart," I told him. "Stanley was brave enough to risk himself for what he thought was right. Others need to do the same."

He sighed and rubbed his leg. "Guess I'm just not as brave."

"I'm not asking you to challenge Dallas or confront him or even leave the pack," I said. "I just want you to visit Stanley, to give him some of the companionship he needs. I think if you'd still be his friend, he'd be okay."

Bart was silent for a long time, then slowly shook his head. "Dallas would find out, and I'd get kicked out of the pack."

"And you'd have a friend in Accident to hunt with, to pal around with," I told him. "It might happen. Dallas might find out, and although my sisters and I are trying to change things in the pack, I can't guarantee that you won't get exiled. But I've got an idea to help keep this all secret, to keep it so no one knows. No guarantees, but I think I can fix it so you can hang out with Stanley at least in a private area where you can talk. And I'll work on something where the pair of you can go hunting on one of the other mountains without getting caught."

His expression turned hopeful. "Really?"

I stood. "Really." Digging in my purse, I pulled out one of my amulets and gave it to him. "No one will see you coming and going from my office while you've got this. Be at my office every Sunday at nine in the morning, and you and Stanley can talk. Heck, I'll even spring for donuts and coffee."

He grinned, then his smile faded. "But what am I going to tell the pack?? They're nosy as all heck here. Someone is going to want to know why I'm going into town every Sunday morning, and, amulet or no, they'll probably follow me if I don't have a good answer."

I told him my plan, then he laughed, tucking the amulet in his pocket and struggling to get to his feet.

"Dang, Bart, how bad did Melvin stab you?" I asked as I handed him a walking stick.

"Clean through my leg," he told me. "Bled all over the place."

I deactivated the silence charm and tucked it back into my pocket before helping Bart to the door. When I opened it, I was glad I'd used the charm because there had to be two dozen werewolves crowded around outside Bart's house, all staring at him with eager anticipation.

"What'd you win in the raffle, Bart?" one shouted.

He stood for a moment, eyeing them all with a smug grin. "Three months of tap dance lessons. Every Sunday morning."

The group sucked in a collective breath, then cheered, all of them excited about Bart's good fortune.

"Congratulations, Bart." One of the werewolves patted him heartily on the shoulder. "Sorry you didn't get that latch-hook rug, but this is almost as good. Tap dancing. Think you'll be any good at it?"

He most certainly would not be any good at it since he wouldn't actually be taking dance lessons on Sunday mornings, but that was part of the plan. No one would think twice when after three months, a werewolf lacked any tap dancing skill whatsoever despite diligent practice and regular lessons. And it wasn't really the dancing that anyone cared about anyway; it was just the fact that he'd been lucky enough to win something in a raffle.

Werewolves loved luck. They loved being lucky more

than anything else in the world. Maybe I could use that to my advantage as a Perkins witch and try to do my part to bring about peace on the mountainside.

But all the great ideas in the world wouldn't do any good if I couldn't manage to do a spell. I only had so many amulets and charms left, and when those were gone, I wasn't sure I'd be able to make more.

Once again, I wondered if I was still a luck witch or not.

CHAPTER 6

SYLVIE

$\mathcal{I}$ headed down the road from the compound, pulling over to the side to let a shiny huge diesel truck edge by me. The truck slowed and stopped even with my car, the window whirring down to reveal a pretty werewolf with blonde hair and a smattering of freckles across a sun-burned nose.

"Sylvie! It's so good to see you. Were you up meeting with Dallas or something?"

I barely knew Tink, so her effusive greeting was a bit puzzling. Yes, she was probably just as gossipy as all the others here in Accident, but I got the impression there was something beyond mere curiosity that made her stop her truck to talk to me.

"I was meeting with Bart," I told her. "He won something in the firehouse raffle."

Her eyes lit up. "Ooh, the latch-hook rug?"

I shook my head. "Tap dance lessons."

She wrinkled her nose. "That's pretty cool too, although everyone wanted that rug."

I sat for a second, waiting for her to tell me why she'd wanted to talk. It didn't take long.

"Um, Sylvie?" The werewolf chewed her bottom lip. "Do you think you can fit me into your schedule sometime next week? Make it all discrete-like because I don't want anybody knowing I'm coming to see you."

I nodded because no one wanted anyone to know they were seeing me. "I've got an opening Tuesday at ten. Does that work?"

She nodded, so I dug into my purse on the passenger seat and pulled out one of my amulets. "Just hold this in your hand when you come, and no one will see you."

She reached out the window to take it and let out a breath, her shoulders relaxing in relief. "Thanks. I'm hoping you can help me out. I promised Dallas some things before we got mated, and he really wants these things, but I've got no idea how to do them. I mean, I read some articles online, but I think they're leaving out a few things."

I tried to remain composed, struggling to keep a professional, mildly interested expression on my face. "Sex?"

She glanced around furtively then nodded. "There's this thing with a lemon zester and hemorrhoid cream, and I don't want to screw it up. Dallas really wants this, and I promised."

Ugh. I had no idea whatever the holy heck Tink was trying to do with a lemon zester and hemorrhoid cream, and I wasn't sure I wanted to know, but I wasn't about to kink shame anyone.

"We'll talk," I promised her.

She grinned. "Awesome. I'll see you on Tuesday at ten."

I waved and started to drive off. "Tuesday at ten."

As I drove down the mountain, I thought about the problem with the werewolves. I thought about the problems the lone wolves were facing. I thought about lemon zester and hemorrhoid cream and wondered how the hell that could possibly be erotic.

And I wondered about Eshu. What was he doing right now? Had he come to deliver messages to Lucien? Would he stop by my house to see me again, or had he forgotten all about me?

* * *

I WAS WANTING nothing more than Glenda's foul smoothie and a nap, but instead I drove out of Accident past the wards and to a building in a neighboring town that housed the law office where Cassie worked.

My sister was in her office, behind a desk with folders stacked so high I could barely see her. She peeked around a folder-tower, then grabbed a handful and moved them to the floor as I sat across from her.

"How are you feeling? You look tired. You should go home and nap, or better yet, go to my house and nap on the couch."

I rolled my eyes. "I'm fine. I plan on taking a nap as soon as I'm done here—at my own house and in my own bed."

She eyed me with concern. "My couch is always open, Sylvie."

I waved the offer away. "I know, and I appreciate it. I popped by to talk to you about the werewolf situation, not my health. I'm worried about the mental and emotional state of the lone wolves in Accident. They're not adapting well to being completely severed from the pack and any contact with other werewolves. I think we need to address this. Maybe find a way to allow werewolves to talk and meet with the lone wolves in town? It won't be the same as hunting with the pack or being permitted on the compound, but at least it will help with the crushing isolation they're feeling."

Cassie sighed and leaned back in her chair. "Sylvie, I'm sympathetic. Believe me, I want the same thing, but there are priorities. De-escalating the conflict between Dallas and Clinton comes first. I can't have a war right now—not in Accident and not on the mountain. I told both werewolves I want them both to meet with me Monday. There's got to be a way to get the pair of them to back off on this fighting. If I can get them to do that, then maybe in a few months, we can talk to them about easing up on the banishments."

"This is important," I told her. "Werewolves are social beings, *pack* beings, and this isolation isn't good for either Shelby or Stanley."

"I don't want to hit Dallas and Clinton with too many demands, too many changes, all at once," she warned me. "Let's see how things go on Monday at the meeting first, then we'll see how fast we can move on this other issue."

I was disappointed, but I understood. Hopefully Cassie getting Dallas and Clinton both in a room would get a cease-fire going and work toward some long-term solution to this mess. Hopefully. I shook my head, doubtful that much was going to come of that meeting.

Cassie was an amazing lawyer, but mediation wasn't her strong point. Actually, it was *my* strong point. Although, I doubted even Nelson Mandela with a fist full of amulets could get those two werewolves to stand down.

And in the meantime, I'd do all I could so that Stanley could at least have a friend to chat with once a week. And maybe, just maybe, if all went well, we could push for something more.

CHAPTER 7

I sat at the bar, turned around so I could see the band, a glass of ginger ale in my hand. I'd gone straight home from Cassie's office, downed a glass of Glenda's smoothie, and napped the afternoon away, waking up around five. While eating my leftover Chinese for dinner, I'd taken stock of my physical stamina and what options I had for the evening. I wasn't about to go back to bed after lying on a couch for two weeks. I needed to get out. I needed to start resuming my normal life so I could get over the physical and emotional trauma of my death. So, after a pep talk and some determined effort, I got a shower, slapped on some makeup, and headed to Pete's to listen to the band.

They were only on song two and already I was realizing this probably wasn't the best idea. I was tired. The day had taken a lot out of me, and the effects of Glenda's smoothie were starting to wear off. My goal of enjoying a night out had quickly turned to sipping my drink, waiting for the band to break, then heading home and to bed.

Despite my exhaustion, I was glad I'd gone out. The band was excellent, and it felt good to be out and about among the townsfolk. There had been three fairies, two harpies, two nymphs, six gnomes, a goblin, a fetch, two minotaurs, a bear shifter, four pixies, and half a dozen werewolves all in the bar when I'd arrived. I was pretty sure by the time I'd left, another twenty of Accident's residents would be packed in, drinking, dancing, and occasionally fighting. Pete tried to keep the peace the best he could, but it was expected that a few brawls would break out during the course of an evening. If things got too out of hand, Pete would come around the bar with the towel Bronwyn had enchanted for him, and the fighters would either take it into the parking lot or play nice. No one wanted to get whacked with a magicked towel. It was Pete's way of keeping the order, and it worked.

Fear the towel.

Right now, the bar was lively but not wall-to-wall people. Everyone seemed to be sober enough that no fights had broken out, although there had been a few words exchanged. As usual, it was the werewolves who were causing the most ruckus, and I glared over at them to see if I knew any of the six well enough to chide them for their rowdy behavior. I recognized three, but not enough for my word to carry any weight with them. It was just as well since I really wasn't in any condition to be confronting werewolves.

The band had just announced their break and I was getting ready to pay for my ginger ale when someone slid into the seat next to me. I looked over and saw a dark-skinned man with a close-cut beard and short curly black hair. He wasn't any taller than me, was average in build, and although his features were attractive, he wasn't what I'd call particularly handsome. But his grin and the sparkle in his brown eyes made my heart skip a beat.

"Eshu. I didn't realize you hung out in town. Are you here for the band?" I asked.

"Nope. I'm here for you. What are you drinking?"

I slid off the stool, my heart rate increasing. "Me? Does Cassie need me for something?" He was a messenger. I figured Lucien had sent him to get me because of an emergency.

"I hope not." He waved down the bartender, then scooted his stool closer. "It took me forever to find you. You weren't at your house when I went by this morning, so I followed your sister around for a few hours, hoping she'd lead me to you. Then I started to search the town. Let me tell you, that sister of yours does some boring stuff. Do you know the majority of her day is spent in a tiny office with stacks of papers?? Reading them. And typing things on a computer. I'd shoot myself. What do you do all day? When you're not lying on a couch, that is?"

I smothered a laugh at his description of Cassie's job. "Well, I sit on a chair and listen to people talk."

He turned, grabbing the two beers from the bartender and passing me one. "That doesn't sound any more exciting than looking at papers. You should definitely consider a different job. Or maybe just stop showing up and do something fun instead like have sex with me."

I rolled my eyes and handed him the beer back. "I can't drink this. I died two weeks ago. I haven't fully recovered from it yet and alcohol probably isn't going to speed that process along."

"You actually died?" He eyed me over, gaze lingering on my chest. "That happens to me *all* the time. How did you die? Did a piano fall on your head? An angry demon rip your guts out? Someone throw you so far up into the sky that you fell into the sun?"

"I was electrocuted while microwaving hot fudge."

His eyes widened. "That's amazing! How many other times have you died?"

I felt like I was getting my second wind, so I grabbed the

beer back from him and took a sip. "None. I only died the once and let me tell you, I really don't want to ever experience it again."

He sighed. "I know. You die as much as I have, and you get kinda used to it though. Death by hot fudge. That's really impressive. Why are you not recovered?"

"Probably because I'm a human and not a demon." I was worried I wouldn't fully recover, that I'd always have this exhaustion, that I'd need to drink Glenda's nasty smoothies every day for the rest of my life just to have some sort of normalcy, but I didn't want to go into all that angst with a guy I was contemplating inviting into my bed.

"You're not really a human, though. You're a witch." He guzzled down the beer and flagged the bartender for another. "I'm not really a demon, although everyone calls me one. I'm not an angel, either. I was born before the demons, before the angels, before the first spark of creation."

"And your job is to deliver messages," I teased.

He shot me a wicked look and spun his empty bottle around on one finger. "And other things. My job is to be Eshu and let me tell you, that is enough of a job for me."

The werewolves a few feet away roared in laughter over something. I'd been trying to ignore them, but it was growing increasingly difficult as the volume of their conversation increased.

They were discussing something about an upcoming fight and how they couldn't wait to kill those who'd left the pack and tried to steal territory from them. One of the wolves mentioned Stanley and Shelby, saying they deserved the same fate, even if they hadn't tried to take territory on the mountain. I stiffened, worried that the two lone wolves might find themselves in danger. Cassie had given them sanctuary in town and had put the force of her magic behind her demand that no one in the wolf pack could harass or bother them.

Was that coming to an end? Was it not just a war on the mountain between two werewolf packs that I needed to be concerned about? Could we be facing a war in the future between the werewolves and the witches?

Eshu spun the bottle around on the tip of his finger again and started singing some bawdy song about a pirate and a prostitute. I tried to tune him out and listen in on the werewolves. Were they planning something? I'd need to figure out what was going on and warn Cassie.

"I don't give a crap about that skank screwing a troll, but the traitor should die," one of the werewolves said. "He was spying on us for Clinton. He shouldn't be getting sanctuary. The witches need to give him back to us to deal with."

I winced. They might be drunk and just talking smack, but just in case, Stanley needed to be warned.

"The mate got pegged by a lass with a cock, Oh-ho bend the cook over—"

"Hush," I hissed to Eshu, leaning toward the werewolves.

"We need to deal with Clinton's group first, then Stanley," another said. "I know Dallas isn't thrilled about killing his only pup, but when your boy disrespects you like that, you need to put him down."

"Rum and blow-jobs and fart on the mainsail, Oh-ho bend the cook over."

"Shhh." I clapped a hand over one ear and tried to focus on the werewolves. It was hard since Eshu was between me and them, and the demon—or whatever he was—kept singing and spinning that bottle on his finger.

"Monday...meeting...agree to whatever... after midnight...every last one of them.... You.... Stanley....rest of us....Clinton."

"With a cock like a cannon and balls like walnuts, the lass

gets poked—oops." Eshu went to give the bottle another spin and it shot off his finger and into the head of one of the werewolves with enough force to knock him forward. At the exact same moment, a minotaur edged by us, a lemon drop shooter in hand.

The werewolf turned around with a snarl and punched whoever he assumed hit him in the head with a beer bottle. His fist collided with the minotaur's snout, pushing him back a pace and spilling the lemon drop shooter. Bellowing, the minotaur slammed the glass into the werewolf's nose and lowered his head. With a toss of his horns, the werewolf flew up and into his buddies.

I'd lived in Accident my whole life. I was no dummy. The moment that beer bottle hit the werewolf, I was trying to get the heck out of there.

"Fight! Fight!" Eshu chanted, a grin on his face. He pumped his fist, elbow knocking over the full bottle of beer the bartender had brought him and spilling it across the bar.

I grabbed his shirt and pulled for him to come with me. The guy had indicated he had a gazillion lives, but that didn't mean I wanted him dying on my watch. He resisted, and I lost my opportunity to escape as other bar patrons closed in to see a minotaur take on six werewolves.

My money was on the minotaur. And a month ago I wouldn't have minded sticking around to see the show. I *was* a luck witch after all, and the chance of a stray punch coming my way, or me being trampled by a group of satyrs or getting a pint of cheap beer poured over my head would normally have been slim to none. But I'd died, and ever since then, luck did not seem to be on my side.

A goblin pressed against me, pushing my back against the hard wooden edge of the bar. I shifted left to keep from being pinned and found myself practically in Eshu's lap. Evidently, the crazy guy thought I *was* trying to get on his lap because he wrapped an arm around my waist and pulled me there, holding me tight.

Annnnd the guy had a hard-on like a fricken flag pole in his pants. I'd thought he was exaggerating about the size of his member, but evidently not from what I could feel shoved against my butt. I squirmed to get off and regretted the motion immediately as he thrust his hips upward, holding my body against his.

"This is turning me on too," he shouted in my ear. "Nothing like a good fight and a witch on my lap to make me want to do the magic mambo."

"We can't do the magic mambo if we're crushed by goblins and werewolves or gored by minotaur horns," I shouted back. "We need to get out of here."

"And miss this? No way! You've died before. One more time won't matter. Although, crushed by minotaurs and werewolves is far less impressive then dying by hot fudge."

Pete came around the corner, towel in hand. I exhaled in relief, knowing it would soon be over. Usually all Pete had to do was snap the towel and everyone settled down, but the minotaur and the werewolves were too busy beating the crap out of each other to notice. Pete shouted, cracking the towel a few times, then went to climb on top of the bar. His foot landed in Eshu's spilled beer and he fell to the ground, his enchanted towel landing on top of my head.

Thankfully Bronwyn had magicked the towel so it didn't work on any of us Perkins sisters or Pete, so it was merely blinding me and filling my nose with the odor of stale beer and greasy hamburger. Didn't Pete ever wash the darned thing? Once this was all over, I was going to have a serious conversation with him about proper care of magical items.

I pushed the towel away from my face just in time to see the minotaur pick up one of the werewolves and throw him across the room. One of his buddies barreled into the minotaur, shoving him back toward me. I yelped, scrambling off Eshu's lap and diving out of the way just as the minotaur crashed against the bar. It cracked. The minotaur tossed his head, and a whole pile of werewolves sailed over the top and into a mirrored wall with whole shelf of booze.

"Eshu!" I shrieked, hoping the guy hadn't used up all his lives because he'd either gotten crushed between a minotaur and a solid oak bar or ended up being smashed into the rail liquor with the werewolves.

"Couch-witch!" he shouted back, popping his head up over the edge of the bar. With a leap that would have done an acrobat proud, he vaulted on top of the bar, stepping on a werewolf's head and one of the minotaur's arms on the way over to jump down.

"Are you a whisky witch or a rum witch?" He stood before me, holding a bottle in each hand as we were being shoved around by the press of the crowd. "I hope you're a rum witch because I'm in a pirate-y mood tonight. Arrrr!"

"I'm about to be a dead witch or, at the very least, a flat witch if we don't get out of here," I shouted. Reaching up to grab the towel off my head, I realized it was no longer there. Ugh. That had been my idea for clearing a path to the door, and now it was probably on the floor being trampled by half a dozen people.

"Don't worry, my beloved couch-witch. I'll save you!" Eshu looked back and forth between the two bottles, then smashed the whisky one over the minotaur's head, clearly deciding the rum bottle was worth saving.

The minotaur roared and flung the werewolves aside as if they were rag dolls, smoke puffing from his nostrils as he focused his rage on Eshu. I screamed, ducking down and trying to find a way through the mob. That's when I saw the towel.

Dropping to my hands and knees, I prayed for my

witchy-luck to return as I scrambled among all the stomping feet and hooves, crawling my way to the bit of white terry cloth I'd spied between two bar stools. Spilled beer and booze dripped down on me, and I stretched out my hand, fingers closing on the towel. Someone grabbed my waist, and I felt myself being dragged backward. With a panicked shriek, I struggled free and started whipping the towel around my head, indiscriminately smacking people in the legs with it. I knew I was nailing lots of innocent people with the thing, but at this point, my main concern was not dying a second time.

Every person I hit went down, legs numb, a glazed expression of confusion on their faces. I was like a tornado clearing a path to the door. When I felt the cool fresh air against my face, I stood, holding on to the door jamb as I looked behind me.

"Pete!" I grabbed a decent-sized rock from beside the door, wrapped the towel around it, and threw it to the bartender. For the first time since my death, my luck held, and the towel-wrapped rock flew right into his hands. Pete shouted for everyone to "settle the ever-loving F down" and started hitting the minotaur and werewolves with the towel, nailing a few goblins who'd joined the fray in the process.

I took a deep breath, ran a shaking hand through my beer-soaked hair and turned, walking smack into Eshu. He steadied me with one hand, his other hand still clutching the bottle of rum.

"You sure know how to show a guy a good time, couch-witch." He held up the bottle. "I haven't had this much fun in…. well, in a few hours. Let's go back to your place, drink this rum, and screw until sunrise."

I maneuvered my way around him and headed to my car. "I'm going back to my place, but I think screwing is not going to happen tonight. If I can manage to get a shower before I collapse into bed, I will. I'm exhausted. I've been crawling around on the floor of a bar. I reek of beer and booze, and my hair is sticky. And I almost died for the second time in my life."

Most people would have blamed Eshu for the bar brawl; after all, he was the one whose spinning beer bottle had started the whole thing, but I'd lived in Accident my whole life. There wasn't a night that went by where there wasn't a fight at Pistol Pete's or somewhere else in the town. This many different supernatural beings all living together was pretty much a powder keg in a room full of lit candles and torches. If it hadn't been Eshu's bottle, it would have been something else. The werewolves were itching for a fight. Someone would have stepped on someone's foot, or flirted with the wrong guy or girl, or insulted one of the fairies, or accidently knocked a goblin over, and the end result would have been the same. Most of the time it was the werewolves, but there were plenty of other feisty, fight-happy creatures who lived here. It was why Pete had Bronwyn make him the towel. And honestly, if he hadn't slipped on the bar and dropped the thing, events would never have gotten as out of hand as they had.

Although now that I thought of it, he *had* slipped on Eshu's spilt booze. It was like bad luck followed the guy around. Maybe that was a bit unfair, though. Everyone had times when things went wrong in their lives. It didn't mean he was a walking hex just because a whole lot went down at his hands tonight. And just because I'd had a twenty-nine-year streak of fortune as a luck witch didn't mean I should expect it to continue. Things had been rocky after my death. It could be that my luck had taken a hit. It could be that my luck would never fully recover. It could be just a blip and things would be back to normal by next week.

Besides, tonight wasn't *totally* bad luck. I did manage to

grab the towel and get out. I didn't get hurt at all. I was fine. So maybe my luck was starting to return, and I just needed to look at things differently.

We both walked to my car. My hand shook on the keys as I tried to beep the lock on my door.

"Here." Eshu handed me the bottle of rum and took the keys, unlocking the door and guiding me around to the passenger side.

"I can drive," I protested. Yes, I was tired and shaky, but it's not like I'd drank anything beyond ginger ale and a sip of beer. Plus, it was only five miles to my house.

Ignoring my objections, Eshu gently got me situated, fastening my seatbelt and doing a thorough job of running his hands along my waist and thighs as he did so. Even as tired as I was, I didn't push him away. His attentions warmed my heart, and his hands were doing a good job of warming other parts of my body as well.

I closed my eyes, resting my head against the back of the seat as he climbed in the driver's side, started my vehicle, and drove. He went straight to my house without needing any directions, running my car up over the curb a bit and into one of my rhododendrons. I didn't care. I was too exhausted to care.

"Lazy couch-witch," he murmured, picking me up and carrying me to my house. Somehow, he managed to get the door open and me inside, depositing me on my couch and covering me up with the afghan after taking my shoes off.

I heard the clink when he put the rum down on the coffee table. Then he leaned over and kissed me on my forehead. "Sure you don't want to screw? I've got a massive tent pole that's got your name all over it."

I smiled with my eyes still closed. "Rain check, Eshu. I'm too tired for that."

"You can just lie there. In fact, if you fall asleep in the

middle of it, that's okay. Although I'm so good in the sack there's no way you'll doze off with me rocking your garden of love."

"Another night," I whispered, wanting nothing more than the joyful oblivion of sleep right now.

"Guess I'll just have to masturbate, then. Oh, and I'm taking the rum."

I murmured something and heard him let himself out, noting the sound of the deadbolt sliding home. That meant he'd taken my keys. Oh, well. I had a spare set, and it was reassuring knowing that I didn't have to get up and stagger over to lock the door. Accident was a safe town if you were a witch, but I still didn't like to take chances. I slept better knowing the doors and windows were all locked, even if I wasn't so paranoid that I needed to set magical wards on them.

I sighed and snuggled into the pillows and afghan, knowing that I'd need to wash the sticky booze and beer residue off of them all tomorrow. It had been a crazy evening —crazy and scary and kind of fun in an exhilarating I'd-almost-gotten-crushed sort of way.

And Eshu... He was trouble with a capital "T." Everything turned upside down when he was around. It was like being on a rollercoaster where I wasn't sure if I was having the time of my life or experiencing the last moments of my life. But he wasn't boring, and he made me laugh, and I never knew what to expect when he was with me.

And his hands on my waist and legs set off all sorts of sparks and sensations I hadn't felt in a very long time. I'd never taken his constant teasing propositions seriously. Normally I wouldn't be interested in a meaningless fling that might complicate things between us. He wasn't serious. I got the impression he was never serious. And I feared casual sex with Eshu, while it would probably be a whole lot of fun, might leave me wanting a commitment that a demon—or whatever he was—could never give.

Heartbreak wasn't something I wanted to risk right now, but friendship with someone fun and crazy who made me forget my troubles? *That* was something I needed. I knew I wouldn't be able to keep things just friends though, because my body wanted to cross that line with the trickster, even though my more sensible brain warned me that way lay danger—big danger.

CHAPTER 8

SYLVIE

I got up the next morning and contemplated burning my couch. The booze and whatever the heck had been on the floor of Pistol Pete's had permeated the upholstery and the whole thing smelled like cat piss if a cat had gone on a bender the night before.

Hoping for the best, I shoved the blankets and pillows into the wash, hosed the whole thing down with Febreze, and went to take a shower, putting my clothes in a plastic bag to deal with later.

The shower felt amazing, and I glided the scrubby all over my skin, inhaling the aroma of vanilla and lavender. When the hot water was beginning to fade to lukewarm, I got out, toweled myself off, and piled my wet hair on top of my head in a clip. Not even bothering with a bathrobe, I headed down to the kitchen naked, opened the cabinet, and pulled out a jug of Glenda's smoothie.

Should I have asked Eshu to stay last night? It was the question that had been running through my brain ever since I'd woken up. Actually, I was pretty sure a few of my dreams had involved him as well. I'd been too tired last night to do much besides crash on the couch, but if he'd stayed, we could have showered together, had a naked breakfast together, gone back in my bedroom after breakfast for round two. Despite all the bawdy jokes and songs and his constant descriptions of his supposedly enormous cock, I got the feeling he'd be really good in bed. He'd be enthusiastic, and fun, and we'd probably laugh as much as we'd orgasm. Maybe that's what I needed in my life right now. It would be a fling, at the most a friends-with-benefits sort of deal. I couldn't see Eshu taking *anything* seriously, let alone a relationship, and I wasn't sure he was really relationship material anyway.

But fun breathless sex with someone who made me laugh, who made me feel more alive than I'd felt even before my death? That might be worth throwing caution to the winds for.

Trying to delay drinking Glenda's smoothie, I picked up my phone and texted Cassie, letting her know that I needed to talk to her. I'd learned not to call since Cassie always picked up when it was one of us, fearing we were in trouble and needed her. Many times, it had been absolutely obvious she'd been in the middle of sex and my call had brought that to a screeching halt. I had no doubt that she'd paused whatever activity she and Lucien were doing on a Saturday morning to check my text, but at least she could see it wasn't an emergency.

I eyed the jug, knowing I needed to just get this over with. Unscrewing the cap, I drank it all down, gagging and choking at the horrible taste. It was bad. It was worse than the other smoothies she'd been bringing me since I'd died. I knew Glenda was concerned, that she was worried I wasn't healing fast enough, but why oh why did her potions have to taste so foul?

I was rinsing the bottle out when I got Cassie's return text telling me she'd meet me at the diner in an hour. Or maybe two hours. She'd text me when she was on her way. I rolled my eyes and smiled, thrilled that she was in love and happy and getting some hot action anytime she wiggled a finger at Lucien.

Would it be the same with Eshu? Probably not. I was pretty sure he'd be up for sex any time I wiggled my finger, but I couldn't see him being as devoted to me as Lucien was to Cassie. I couldn't see him being as devoted to anyone or anything. It's just how he was. Lighthearted. Fun. Casual. Could I do casual, or would my heart end up wanting more?

I shook off the thoughts and headed upstairs to get dressed, invigorated by Glenda's potion. Cassie might be heading to the diner in an hour or two, but I was heading over now. Why cook breakfast and eat alone when two blocks away I could get an omelet with swiss and bacon and enjoy the reassuring feeling of being surrounded by the good folk of Accident?

Dressed and heading out, I nearly stepped on a note tucked partially under my door mat.

Your office at 8am Saturday. Please.

Sometimes my clients had emergencies. As much as I wanted that omelet, it was going to have to wait. We didn't have a hotline in town or a backup therapist, and many residents either didn't have cell phones or weren't in a position where a phone call would be unheard. Too many of the beings in our town had supernatural hearing, and many of my clients had matters of a sensitive and confidential nature to discuss. So, I tried to make myself available whenever someone needed me.

Stuffing the note into my pocket, I walked past the diner with its tantalizing smells and to my office where I found a werewolf waiting for me—a werewolf who, thanks to my charm, only I could see. We'd had several sessions over the last few months, and I knew he'd been eager to resume and get on my appointment book once I'd come back after my death experience, but I was pretty sure I knew what his emergency was today.

"Sylvie." He shifted nervously, looking down the street. "Thanks for meeting me. It's late notice, I know."

I opened the door and let him in, motioning him toward a chair as I took a seat opposite him. "How are things going, Clinton?"

He looked down and ran a hand over the carved wood of the chair arm. "I did what you said and picked out the rugs, upholstery, and throw pillows for my pack's lodge. Even got a nice shabby-chic accent light for the side table."

"How did that make you feel?" I asked.

He let out a whoosh of breath. "Good. Like it's home. Like it's mine. Just being there calms and centers me. That's not why I wanted to see you, though. There's a meeting coming up on Monday between Dallas and me with your sister there. I need to talk about that."

I nodded. "That meeting will be a huge test of your newfound calm, Clinton. Have you been practicing the techniques we went over? Planning strategies for when you feel like your temper might get out of hand?"

"No. I mean, yes, but that's not it." He fidgeted in the chair. "The meeting is a waste of time. Dallas ain't gonna ever let me have a separate pack inside the wards, let alone on what he feels is his mountain. He ain't gonna budge. Cassie's gonna get mad and lay down the law and try to force what she wants. Nothing constructive is gonna happen. Dallas's wolves already took a quarter mile of what we carved out for our pack, and I know he plans on standing his ground and attacking us the night after the meeting."

I thought of the conversation in the bar last night. "Do

you think he'll offer you a chance to return to his pack and re-integrate?"

Clinton shook his head. "I doubt it. He'd lose face. At this point, it's gone on too long to brush off as just a spat between father and son. I've indirectly challenged him and to let me back in would show weakness on his part. Plus, I'd always be considered a threat. His only offer will probably be for me and my pack to leave the town wards and become exiles in the outside world."

I thought for a moment. "He's got to be feeling just as trapped by all this as you are. I know he cares about you, Clinton. He's just angry and embarrassed and not thinking of creative options for compromise."

The werewolf leaned forward. "This is why we need you there, Sylvie. Not your sister Cassie, but you. That's why I left the note and asked you to meet me. You're discreet. You understand our culture. You've got patience and mediation skills, and with you we could work toward some sort of consensus. With Cassie heading that meeting, it's going to be a disaster."

"Cassie is a lawyer," I reminded him. "I appreciate your faith in my abilities, but she's perfectly capable of mediating between your two packs. Additionally, she's got the power to keep the peace if things get heated *and* to put her foot down if either one of you isn't negotiating in good faith. She's head witch. This is her job."

"Magic aside, you're better at this sort of thing," Clinton told me. "Actually, the fact you can do all those things without using any magic means Dallas is less likely to let his ego get him in trouble."

"I'll talk to Cassie about this," I told him. "But it's her circus and her monkeys. Ultimately it's her decision."

Clinton stood. "Understood. I don't need to be an oracle like Ophelia to see how this is going to end, though."

I stood as well and walked him to the door. "How do you *want* it to end, Clinton? What's your best-case scenario at the end of this issue?"

He shrugged. "We get part of the mountain and recognition as a separate pack. There's no exile, no friction between the two packs. I want my wolves to be able to visit and spend time with family on the other side of the mountain without getting killed, and the same the other way."

"And Shelby? And Stanley?" I asked, hopeful that Clinton had a reconciliation in mind for them as well.

The werewolf's face twisted in anger. "Shelby nearly killed me and she's screwing a troll. And Stanley is a traitor. It's his fault I had to pay for Bronwyn's truck and trailer and that Cassie burned my beard clean off my face."

I kept my mouth shut about the fact that he'd obviously found being beardless an improvement as he was standing before me as clean-shaven as a werewolf could be. And as for him blaming Stanley for all that...well, I was disappointed at this regression. We'd been working on accepting personal responsibility for actions, but clearly the werewolf wasn't ready to claim this one as his own darned fault.

"Take a deep breath and think logically about what would have happened if Stanley had kept his mouth shut," I told him in a calm, even voice.

Clinton did as I said, then scowled. "Ophelia probably would have divined who was behind it, or one of you would have made a truth charm, and I would have had more than my beard burned off. But he's still a traitor and Shelby is still a troll-lover."

I stifled a sigh, knowing when to call it quits for now. It all came down to pride and ego and centuries of tradition and culture with these werewolves. Rome—or Accident—wasn't built in a day, though.

"You do realize that times are changing? Both packs are

going to have to reconsider a good number of their rules and practices, and align with the rest of Accident. This break-out pack you've put together won't be exempt from that, even if we manage to get Dallas to agree to let you guys stay on the mountain."

He took a breath, his fingers on the door handle. "It ain't gonna be easy, Sylvie. Not for any of us. We're used to taking the law into our own hands, and there are some crimes we consider a whole lot more serious than the rest of you do. It's gonna be a problem if those crimes are suddenly not enforced or given a slap on the wrist."

I reached out to pat his shoulder. "I know, Clinton. I really think we can work it out, though. All we need is time, patience, and to communicate honestly with each other."

His smile held a tinge of sadness. "I hope you're right, Sylvie. I hope you're right."

* * *

I POURED a swirl of ketchup on top of my hash browns as Cassie sipped her coffee.

"I can't believe you went to Pistol Pete's last night," she scolded. "You just got back to work, just went back to your house, and instead of taking it easy, you're out partying it up in a bar."

"I felt good and I wanted to hear the band. I wasn't 'partying it up.' I was sitting on a barstool, drinking ginger ale, and listening to the music."

"And finding yourself smack in the middle of a fight," she shot back. "Pete's is trashed. He's making noises about pressing charges against that minotaur and the werewolves. The whole lot of them are squashed into a jail cell right now. You're lucky you got out of there without being trampled or gored or clawed."

I sincerely hoped our sheriff hadn't put the minotaur in the same jail cell as the werewolves. I tried to remember the layout of the jail from the one time I'd been there on a fourth-grade field trip and was pretty sure there had been more than one cell.

"I was fine, Cassie. I'm not a fragile doll; I'm a witch. I grew up here. I know to get out of the way when werewolves and minotaurs start exchanging blows."

She sucked in a breath, stabbing at her pancakes with her fork. "Two weeks ago I almost lost you, Sylvie. I can't lose you. I can't lose any of you. I can't."

Her voice wobbled. Cassie had never been a client of mine. She hadn't needed to be one. We'd grown up together. Sisters. I knew the demons she lived with, and I wasn't talking about the hot one in her bed, either. Our father had taken off and that had been hard enough, but she was thirteen when we'd lost our grandmother, and our mother had left without a word soon after. Loss. Abandonment. The fear that one day she'd wake up and someone else she loved would be gone. We all struggled with these feelings, but Cassie the most. Probably because at thirteen she'd become the legal guardian of six younger sisters and spent most of her life trying to raise us, trying to keep us all safe and sound, and the whole time dealing with her grief and loss alone.

I reached out and took her hand. "Cassie, you did good. We all grew up with food in our bellies and love in our hearts. I had the best childhood, all because of you. But we're grown now. Every one of us is an adult living our own life. The town is your only child to care for and fuss over, at least until Lucien puts a bun in your oven. Let the six of us be adults. Let us walk by your side and stand with you as grown witches who all want to do our part to take care of this town and make it the best it can be for every single resident here."

She nodded, gripping my hand tight. "But if I were to lose one of you…"

"People die. That's a valid fear and one you need to acknowledge. But you can't allow it to consume you and direct your actions."

She took a deep breath. "Dad. Grandma. Mom. I'm sometimes waiting for the other shoe to drop and tragedy to strike, and the panic overwhelms me. But you're right. I trust that a twenty-nine-year-old woman knows if she's recovered enough to go listen to some music at a bar. And that she has enough sense to get the heck out of the way when a fight breaks out."

I smiled. "And here's the part where I tell you I had to crawl along the floor, using Pete's enchanted towel to clear a path to the door."

Cassie groaned. "Not helping, Sylvie. Not helping at all."

I laughed. I don't know why I didn't tell her about Eshu being there, how he'd kinda sorta started the whole thing, how he drove me home when I was too exhausted to unlock my own car door, how he'd tucked me into a blanket on my sofa.

How he'd shown up the night before and pretty much done the same thing.

I didn't tell her. Maybe because I knew deep down she didn't approve of the demon—or whatever the heck he was. Maybe because I knew she wouldn't approve of me having a brief no-strings-attached fling with the guy.

My heartbeat sped up at the thought. It so wasn't me to do something like that, but the thought of a fun, wild, crazy night with Eshu was increasingly appealing.

I let go of Cassie's hand and dug into my omelet and hash browns. "Anyway, right before the fight broke out, I heard the werewolves talking. It may have been a bunch of drunk bravado, but I'm concerned."

My sister swallowed a bite of pancake and shot me a wry smile. "Let me guess—they're going to raid Clinton's territory and kill them all, then they'll grab their torches and pitchforks and head into town to take out Stanley and Shelby."

When Cassie put it that way, it did sound like a bunch of drunken werewolves just spouting off. But it had worried me then and it worried me now.

"I have it from another source that Dallas plans to attack Clinton Monday night after your meeting, regardless of how it goes," I told her, purposely leaving out Clinton's name as my source.

Cassie bit her lip. "That might be the case. I'm really not sure what to do, Sylvie. I can try to get them to come to a peaceful solution. I can threaten them both. But ultimately, if they attack and kill each other, all I can do is support Sheriff Oakes as he investigates and enforces the laws of Accident."

It would result in a lot of werewolves, including Dallas, being expelled from the protection of the wards and might serve as a deterrent against any action in the future, but that wouldn't help those who died, and it would set the remaining werewolves against the town in a huge feud that would last centuries. No, letting the two packs duke it out wasn't the solution. I just wasn't sure what was.

"What about the threat on Stanley?" I asked, shifting to the other thing I'd heard last night.

"That one I have more faith on. Bronwyn and I can work on some additional protections for Stanley's place, and I'll even ask Sheriff Oakes to assign a deputy to watch his house Monday night. Plus, Dallas knows that any action his pack members make on a lone wolf will come back on him. I'll hold him personally responsible, and I made it very clear that if he pissed me off enough, if he disrespected the rule of law here, he was going to end up outside the town wards at best, dead at worst. He might risk that to take out a rival pack as he considers the mountain to be his territory, but he won't have the same excuse for attacking a werewolf under my protection in the town proper."

I felt the undercurrent of anger in Cassie's voice, saw the spark in her eyes. She's always had issues controlling her temper, and she absolutely had the power to make those threats a reality. It wasn't just that my eldest sister was a lawyer, she'd always dealt with conflict with a firm authoritative hand. I'm not saying that didn't have its place in our world, but in my opinion, Cassie often jumped in with her mandates and threats of force when there was still opportunity for compromise and a peaceful solution—a peaceful solution that didn't involve setting an ex-boyfriend's pants on fire in the middle of the courthouse, or burning off Clinton Dickskin's beard or possibly forcing Dallas Dickskin outside the town wards in exile.

"What's your plan for Monday's meeting?" I asked, worried what her answer would be.

"I let both packs lay their demands on the table. We discuss what's acceptable and what's not acceptable from the point of view of Accident as a whole, then they hash out the rest between them."

I tried hard to keep my expression neutral. Luckily, I had years of professional experience doing this. I also knew that Cassie liked to hear things straight and not dance around an issue. For all her temper, she was readily swayed by a solid argument and was truly willing to see another's point of view.

"I'm about to suggest something, and you're not going to like it," I warned her.

Her eyes searched my face, then she leaned back with a sigh. "No. You're not mediating this in my stead."

I bit back a smile, because she knew me so well. Only

Ophelia knew me better, and she was my twin. "I'm very concerned that this situation is a powder keg. While your style of conflict resolution has merit and has a key place in the governing of Accident, I feel it's too early in the mediation process to force a solution. I love you, Cassie. Accident is a safe place because if the crap hits the fan, you are absolutely capable of taking out the trash. But we're not at that point yet with the werewolves, and I worry that sending in the heavy artillery is going to make a tricky situation a whole lot worse."

She glared at me. "I hate it when you talk sense, you know. I hate it when you sit there all calm and gently tell me I'm not the right witch for this job and do it in a way that has me agreeing with you."

I laughed. "That's what I do, Cassie. Every day of my job. That's what I do. And that's why I need to be at this meeting Monday."

"With me?"

The very fact that she'd framed that as a question meant she already knew the answer.

"Do you think that's a good idea? Will your presence will help or hurt the negotiations?"

She sighed. "Hurt. It will be hard for you to keep things calm and de-escalate any tension with me sitting there ready to burn beards and pants off werewolves. I'm just scared, Sylvie. I know you're good, and you're a grown woman who is fully capable of sitting in a room with angry werewolves and getting them to talk about their feelings and crap like that. But I'm worried. You almost got squashed last night in a bar. You couldn't calm that situation. I'm concerned the same thing is going to happen in this meeting."

"There won't be a minotaur at this meeting," I reminded her. "Or booze. Dallas and Clinton won't be there to drink and get rowdy; they're there to have their positions heard and validated, and discuss options." I rolled my eyes at her skeptical expression. "If it makes you feel any better, I'll take Pete's towel."

She chuckled. "I'd rather you take Lucien but having him there would probably get everyone's fur up just as much as having me there. Besides, he's had to run off to hell and he might not be back for a day or two."

"I'll be fine on my own," I assured her. "I'm a luck witch, remember? And my job is to guide people to a better understanding of themselves and each other."

"And to expand their sexual horizons into a really kinky direction." Cassie grinned. "Just remember to bring some luck charms, okay? And promise me you'll be okay. If things start to go south, get the heck out of there and I'll drive up that mountain the next day and take care of it myself."

Luck charms. My heart sank at the thought of the spell items sitting on my counter, waiting for me to work on them. Was I strong enough yet? I did feel better today than I had since the accident, but was it enough? Could I put something together in time for Monday's meeting? Was I even a luck witch anymore?

I kept my expression neutral. "I promise. I'm good at this, Cassie. It's my thing. Have some faith in my ability to guide the werewolves toward a peaceful solution."

Cassie poked at the few bites of pancake left on her plate and shook her head. "I have absolute faith in you, Sylvie. It's the werewolves I don't trust."

I thought of Clinton in my office this morning, of Shelby yesterday with Alberta, of all the werewolves I'd seen over the years. This was the difference between Cassie and me. She saw them as a defense attorney would. She saw them through the lens of a member of the legal system, as the witch responsible for everyone in Accident. I saw them as complex individuals with hopes and dreams and struggles, just like everyone else in this town. I respected them. I respected their culture. And I knew that deep down inside, every one of them wanted the same thing we all did—peace, joy, love, and friendship.

Hopefully I was the right witch to help them achieve those things.

CHAPTER 9

SYLVIE

*A*fter brunch I swung by the firehouse to see Ophelia. She generally worked Thursday through Saturday and the occasional Sunday, so outside of family dinners we tended to get together early in the week for lunch or dinner. Now that Nash was in her life, I'd expected our weekly get togethers to turn into more like monthly get togethers, but so far, she'd made sure to continue our routine. I appreciated it. I would have completely understood if a new boyfriend took priority. Love was a bit all-consuming and burned hot and heavy early in a relationship, and I knew how important it was for them to spend time getting to know each other, turning what might have just been attraction and infatuation into something long-term.

But she was my twin. There was a bond between us that was different than what we shared with our other sisters. Plus, she was the reason I was alive. Nash had fallen in love with her and offered to resurrect me, sacrificing his life as a reaper in the process. It tied me to her even more. And I would be forever grateful to Nash for what he'd done, even though I knew he did it for Ophelia and not me. Still, he'd brought me back to life and that meant I was most definitely Team Naphelia—or should that be Team Ophash—when it came to the couple.

Ricky was sitting in front of the firehouse. The bear shifter had his feet spread out in front of him, hands resting on top of his round belly. On the ground next to him was a big glass of lemonade, which I was pretty sure had more sugar than lemon juice in it. Ricky had a sweet tooth. That plus his belly had earned him the nickname of Pooh-bear. Personality-wise, it fit as well. He had a sweet smile, warm, lazy brown eyes and a relaxed way of dealing with life. He approached an emergency with the same cheerful, competent calm as he did everything else. I liked him, but then I liked all of Ophelia's coworkers. Actually, I liked everyone in Accident. No matter who they were, I always saw something in even the grumpiest shifter, self-centered vampire, or vain fairy to respect.

"Is Ophelia in?" I asked Ricky.

He waved toward the back room. "She's in charge of food this week."

I grimaced, because in our family Glenda was the only one to inherit the gourmet gene. Cassie was a decent cook if it was something simple. Bronwyn had one or two staples she'd managed to get down pat. Adrienne could pretty much only make pie. The rest of us relied on packaged food and carry-out.

"So, what's on the menu for tonight then?" I shot him a sympathetic glance.

"Boxed macaroni and cheese. I think she's going to put bacon in it. Last night was tuna casserole."

"Also out of a box?"

He nodded. "That's Ophelia. Thursday was chili out of a can, so we're stepping up in the world tonight."

I looked through the firehouse to the back room. "Why's

she in the kitchen now? It's not even noon. It can't take even Ophelia five hours to cook bacon and boil water for macaroni."

"Dishes from breakfast," he told me. "She made pancakes. The kind that come in a bottle where you just add water and shake it up, then pour it onto a griddle. At least the coffee wasn't instant."

We could all manage coffee, thankfully. "Too bad Nash can't cater your food. He's working at the diner, you know."

Ricky chuckled. "Nash's job right now is cutting vegetables and flipping burgers. I'm not sure a reaper's culinary skills are much better than your sister's. Next week it's Brandy's turn, so we'll just have to hang on until then and try not to starve to death."

The sylph was vegan, but she was a darned good cook. And I knew she tried to prepare food that appealed to her meat-loving coworkers. Last time I'd stopped by, she'd made some eggplant dish that was one of the best things I'd ever eaten outside of Glenda's cooking.

I headed in through the firehouse and found Ophelia in the kitchen, drying a pan. Her smile when she saw me lit up her face. She stuck the pan in a cabinet, then came over and gave me a hug. "What's up, Syl?"

For some reason, I felt overcome with emotion and hugged her tight, blinking back tears. "I just wanted to see you. Bounce a few things off you. Maybe see if you had any insight into a few issues I'm dealing with."

She gently disengaged from my hug, her eyes searching mine. "Everything okay? You're feeling all right? Not pushing it too hard so soon after your accident, are you?"

I'd hid my lingering exhaustion and fears from Cassie and the others, but not Ophelia. There were few things I could ever hide from my twin.

"I'm tired but getting stronger each day. Glenda's

smoothies are helping, and honestly I think it's good for me to get back to work and be in my own house and bed again." I headed over to the long table where the firehouse staff ate and sat down, Ophelia taking a seat by my side. "I'm struggling with my magic though," I confessed. "And I don't feel... well, as lucky as I normally feel."

Ophelia ran a hand down my arm and gripped my fingers in hers. "It's only been two weeks. You almost died. Give it some time and everything will be back to normal."

"I *did* die," I shot back, then gave my sister an apologetic smile. "Sorry. It's just that I'm frustrated and scared. What if being dead did something to my magic? What if I'm always tired and weak, and I've permanently damaged something in my abilities?"

"You want me to do a reading? Scry? Is that what you came to ask me?" Ophelia gently prodded. "You know my divinations aren't always clear, but I can try to see what the future holds for you."

I nodded. "There's a lot going on, and I'm feeling like someone stuck me in a dryer and turned it on high. The accident. My physical health. My magic. And then there's this thing with the werewolves. I told Cassie that I want to mediate the meeting on Monday to try to see if I can get them to come to an agreement without us witches needing to play the heavy. Then there's..." I hesitated, not sure if I wanted to admit that I was considering a fling with Eshu or not. At twenty-nine, I felt like I shouldn't be contemplating what would basically be a hook-up and talking it up with my twin. Plus, I knew Lucien wasn't a fan of Eshu, and thus neither was Cassie. Ophelia had never met him, but I was sure her opinion would be colored by whatever Cassie had told her over the last few weeks.

I didn't want to face her incredulous comments about my thinking of having a fling with a demon that everyone thought was a frivolous screw-up. If I did decide to go there, it would probably end up being just a one-night stand. No need for anyone to know about it. No need for Ophelia to know about it.

Yes, the therapist in me was shaking her head that I was thinking of having a sexual relationship, no matter how brief, with someone that I would be too ashamed to admit having slept with. That was all sorts of wrong, but I had far too many issues going on right now to go into a deep self-analysis on why I was attracted to someone who my family would most certainly not approve of, and why at almost thirty I didn't have the courage to do what I wanted without worrying about my family's opinions on the matter.

"My health, my magic, and the werewolf issue," I repeated. "That's what I need a divination on."

Ophelia gave me an odd look, then got up and made me a cup of coffee, adding a little dash of milk, just as I liked.

"Reading tea leaves now?" I joked. "Or coffee grounds?"

"Nope. Just getting you settled in and relaxed while I get my cards." She slid the coffee across the table to me. "Drink. I'll be back in a second."

I leaned back in the chair, cradling my coffee in my hands. The firehouse kitchen was cheery, the walls painted a light blue, the cabinetry a glossy white. The appliances were stainless steel, and someone had purchased towels and dishes in blue jewel tones that tied everything together in a calming palette straight out of a decorating magazine. I breathed deep, exhaling through my mouth and taking the occasional sip of coffee. By the time Ophelia returned, I felt more centered than I had in weeks.

"That's better." She smiled and sat across from me, shuffling her deck of cards and handing them to me. I divided them into three piles. With a steady breath, I turned over the first card.

The Tower. I grimaced because this wasn't my first rodeo when it came to Ophelia's divinations. I knew this card and I knew what it meant. The only good thing was it was in the past position of my reading and not the present or the future.

"Past events that are still affecting you. These things could be holding you back or providing a foundation that your future will be built upon."

"Destruction. Chaos. Massive unexpected change." I reached out a finger to touch the image of a lightning-shattered building, two people falling headfirst from the heights. It wasn't lost on me that the very force of nature destroying the tower on the card was what had killed me two weeks ago.

"That's the obvious interpretation," Ophelia told me. "That your electrocution has been a dramatic and chaotic change in your life and that it's affecting both your present and your future. But there's always more to a reading than what's at face value. The tower falls not just because of the lightning strike, but because it's built on an unstable ground of false truths and illusions. The lightning serves as a bolt of insight. It levels the tower and provides the space for a stronger and more stable growth. As traumatic as this change is, it creates an environment for equally dramatic development."

I nodded, understanding what Ophelia was saying, but not sure how my death two weeks ago would lead to something positive. For Ophelia, maybe. My accident had brought Nash fully into her life in a way that he never would have been able to be before. But a clearing to prepare for growth? I just didn't see that, especially since I was still feeling weak and my magic wasn't working as it had been before I'd died microwaving hot fudge.

"You have to surrender to this, Sylvie," she told me. "No matter how hard it is, no matter how impatient you are for things to return to the way they were before, you need to let it all be. You need to be prepared to accept a new reality and build your life on new foundations, not old ones."

I sucked in a breath, not liking that one bit. I wanted things to go back to the way they were before the accident. I wanted to not feel like I needed two naps a day. I wanted to have my powers back, to win raffles, and always find a good parking spot at the mall and manage to arrive at the post office right before they closed. I didn't want my world to change. I wanted it to stay the same. And from all the clients I'd counseled in my life, I knew how sometimes that just didn't happen.

With barely concealed anxiety, I turned over the next card.

The Fool.

"Beginnings. New opportunities. You're at a point where you need to follow your heart, to put aside anxious thoughts and both commit and walk forward in faith."

Ophelia's voice faded into the background as I stared at the card. I knew what the Fool signified but looking at the cheerful man with his little white dog and his knapsack over his shoulder, with his one foot poised to step over a cliff— looking at that card, all I saw was Eshu.

He was the embodiment of The Fool—a being that lived strictly by intuition, that enjoyed and relished every moment of life. He was someone who took life's bumps and treated them as if they were a thrill-ride, a roller-coaster. My present card might have signified new beginnings as far as Ophelia's interpretation was concerned, but I knew that this card meant that whatever my future held, Eshu in my present was instrumental in bringing that future to fruition.

My hand hovered over the third card—my future card— and I hesitated.

"This is the outcome of your present. It's what the

clearing of your past and the new beginning of your current state will bring about," Ophelia told me.

Still I hesitated. "I'm hoping it's not the Death card. I've had enough of that to last me for five or six decades."

"The Death card doesn't mean actual death," Ophelia scolded. "It's a card about transformation. It's about shedding your past life for a new life. Given what happened, I think it would be logical for you to draw that card."

Maybe in the past. Or in the present. I didn't want death in my future, even if it was about transformation and new life. I was done with that shit. Right now, I wanted the calm comforting familiarity of my old life, my routines, and daily habits.

Exhaling, I turned over the card. And blinked.

"Oh, that's an excellent omen, Sylvie! Your future is all about finding balance within yourself. You might be uncertain about a direction you might take but trust yourself to make the correct decision. Sometimes the difficult path is the right one, so choose with your heart and you'll find your joy."

I was only half listening to her reading because I was busy staring at the card and making my own interpretation of its meaning.

The Lovers. Kindred spirits. Soulmates. Romance, passion, an intense bond with deep connection. That all sounded awesome, especially to a woman whose romances to date had been best summed up by the word "meh." I couldn't see *all* that in my near future, but I could see some of it.

Passion. Lovers. The moment I'd turned the card over, my thoughts immediately went to Eshu. I was attracted to him and more than just physically. He was fun, exciting. Everything inside me came alive when I saw him. For two weeks, I'd been wondering if sex with him would be as electrifying and entertaining as just being near him. I knew he would be up for that sort of thing, but I'd held back, fearing I would end up far too attached while he remained The Fool, the fun and frivolous guy who never thought past the next day.

Maybe it was time for me to take a chance. Maybe I needed to go down the difficult but ultimately rewarding path and screw this demon's brains out. I'd *died*. Surely that meant I had full karmic permission for some amazing no-strings-attached sex.

And maybe, just maybe, I was wrong about Eshu and he wasn't as frivolous as I'd assumed.

"You okay, Sylvie?"

I looked up to see my twin regarding me with a concerned frowny-face.

"Ophelia? Have you ever said, 'screw it' and had sex with someone who was so very wrong, but who you knew would be an absolute amazingly fun lay?"

Her eyebrows shot up. "You mean like doing it with a reaper less than twenty-four hours after your twin sister nearly died? A reaper you pretty much just met? One who killed your basil plant and spent the night on your couch watching infomercials and porn?"

I laughed. "Point taken, but at least you knew Nash loved you. He saved me. As long as you were willing, he was going to be right there by your side forever. He wasn't some crazy silly make-you-laugh playboy who might be gone the next morning without even a thank you."

Ophelia sucked in a breath. "Oh, God. Please tell me you're not thinking of sleeping with Marcus?"

"No!" I actually recoiled at the suggestion. Cassie's ex was a panther shifter, totally hot and totally unfaithful. Yes, he'd hit on all of us, and yes, we'd all turned him down even after they'd broken up.

Ophelia peered at me, and I could tell by the odd haze over her eyes that she was using her magic. "Seriously? Not that idiot demon that Cassie and Lucien complain about all the time."

"He's not an idiot," I protested. "Have you seen him? He's totally hot, and he makes me laugh. Don't I deserve a little fun?"

Ophelia held up her hands. "Of course you do. It's just that Cassie says Lucien hates him, and she doesn't seem to think very highly of him, either. You've had a really rough couple of weeks, Sylvie. I don't want you to do anything you'll regret later."

I rolled my eyes. "First, Lucien hates Hadur as well, and everyone told him to just deal when Bronwyn brought him home. As I remember, he wasn't too fond of Nash, either. His opinion shouldn't weigh too heavily in my choices of a romantic partner, in my opinion. Secondly, weren't you just doing a reading for me, telling me to take the path my heart wanted, and that although it might be a difficult path, it was the right one?"

My sister stared at me for a moment, then laughed. "Okay. You're right. Screw the hot playboy demon and have an absolute blast doing it. Please know that I'm here with ice cream, wine, and boxes of tissues if it all falls apart."

I knew she would be—all my sisters would be, but especially my twin Ophelia.

"Is that a vision? The falling apart thing? Or just you worrying over me in a similar but different way than Cassie worries over all of us?"

My twin grinned. "The latter. I've got no idea where this thing is going. My love-dar doesn't seem to be working right now, so I can't give you my magical intuition about it all. But I've seen how things go with these fun-frivolous guys, and I know you, Sylvie. I know you love guys who are little boys at heart, who make you laugh. I also know that those guys have never stuck around the way you've wanted them to. I worry this is going to end up the same."

She was probably right, but at this time in my life, I needed to laugh, to forget about my death and the shit-show that was the werewolf issue in our town. And I needed some crazy, fun sex to lift my spirits. Eshu offered both, and I was really wanting to take him up on that offer. I was going to do it. The next time I saw him, whether it was in two days, two weeks, or two months, I was going to get that demon into my bed.

I thought of the reading, then I thought of what I did in my therapy practice. Maybe Ophelia and I weren't so different after all. Twins.

I thanked Ophelia, gave her a hug, and walked through town to my house. Back home I took a nap, then, feeling a bit more energized, I sat down to work on luck charms to give a little help to the mediation on Monday.

There'd been a few months when I'd been all about four leaf clovers cast in resin, or dyed rabbits' feet keychains that I used to buy online in bulk. I'd gone through a phase where I learned metal casting and made coins to use as my charms.

Lately I'd been into buttons. I haunted online yard sales and flea markets where people were trying to unload cigar boxes full of buttons that they'd found after their grandmother or aunt had died. There was something magical about running my fingers through all the different sizes and colors and selecting the ones I wanted. The luck charms I was going to work on were to be for the mediation between Dallas and Clinton, so I searched my boxes of buttons for ones that inspired understanding, affection, and a sense of calm. I intended on putting these charms at the four corners of the room, suffusing the whole area with my magic rather than targeting the individuals.

Plastic buttons with four holes called to me. I selected six for each charm in shades of blue and green, adding a yellow button at the end to inspire creative solutions. Then I strung them onto fine wool yarn, chanting as I worked. When they were completed, I surveyed my handiwork, pleased at the result. They were perfect in every way except for one—they lacked power.

As they were, someone would practically have to hang them from their forehead to get even a minimal bit of the desired result. They needed to be energized with my magic, but that was something I'd lacked since my death. I was exhausted just from putting the charms together, and I knew I was magically tapped out. Was this the way it would always be? I had the skill, the talent, but not the strength to really work my magic? I looked over at a handful of charms I'd been working on last month. They were faded, almost spent. But even month--old charms had more power to them then these ones I'd just made.

What would I do if this was my new normal? My clients relied on my charms to come and go discreetly. What if I could no longer provide that? I was sure some of my clients would stop coming to therapy rather than risk being seen.

And what would I be without my magic? I was still a witch, but I'd be useless. My powers would be so faint that they'd not be of value at all.

It scared me. Setting the charms aside, I packed up my supplies and decided to put the issue in the back of my mind and enjoy myself tonight. It had been weeks since my friends and I had our last game, and I missed it. I wanted to just have fun, eat pizza, hang out with everyone, and worry about my magic later. I'd try to power the charms again tomorrow morning, and if I still couldn't manage, then I'd need to talk to my sisters.

I'd need to talk to Cassie. I knew if I did the technical side of the charms, she could power them for me, but I'd been reluctant to admit I was having this problem. She was hovering over me as it was, fussing about whether I was healed enough to be off her couch, out of her house, and back to work yet or not. Admitting this would make her want to haul me back to her house to take care of me. And admitting my fears of this being permanent would be worse. I didn't want my sisters to think me broken. I didn't want them feeling as if they had to spend their lives taking care of me. I didn't want anyone feeling sorry for me, talking about their abilities in hushed tones, not wanting me to feel bad over not being able to work magic any more.

Rubbing my hands over my face, I took a deep breath and decided to take another quick nap. I headed back to my bedroom and set the alarm on my phone, knowing I'd need to keep my second nap to under a few hours so I had time to get up and ready everything for tonight's game.

And with my mind on my lack of magic and Monday's mediation with the werewolves, I fell into a fitful sleep.

CHAPTER 10

SYLVIE

"*R*oll for initiative," I said.

Immediately the sound of dice on my wooden table drowned out the background classic rock. This was the other me, the one my clients and my family didn't ever see. I'd gotten into role playing games, or RPGs, in college and missed them so much that two years ago I'd started a game of my own. Due to the variety of supernatural beings in Accident, I'd needed to develop my own rules and ended up running a mashed-up version of Dungeons and Dragons, Warhammer, Call of Cthulhu, and RuneQuest.

"Dang it!" John the Cyclops shouted. "My dice are cursed. Someone cursed my dice."

"No one cursed your dice, John," I told him. "Trust me, I could tell."

He eyed me. With his one eye. "If I paid you, could you charm them? So I can roll better?"

That was greeted with howls of protest from the other players.

"No spelled dice," I reminded him. "And that includes

mine, too. We're here to have fun, John. There are no bad rolls." I looked over at his dice. "Well, at least in initiative, there are no bad rolls."

"Everyone is going to be dead before I can use my scroll," he complained. "Can I switch with someone else and go in their place instead?"

Being a game master was like being God, and I certainly had the ability to grant that request. But I chose not to.

"Sorry, John."

"Dude, just chill. Wait your turn. It's not like you have to save us or anything." Smoke curled from Fernando's nostrils. The dragon was in human form right now because he just didn't fit in my dining room or at my table as a giant winged reptile.

Fernando had been through three characters this campaign because he couldn't seem to understand that his human fighter, or half-elf, or human paranormal historian couldn't fly, or spit fire, or eat an entire army. We were working on this inability to see the world from others' eyes, but in the meantime, we'd rolled up a robot fighter that was a bit more able to withstand Fernando's impulsive actions.

"Flora, you're up," I told the Valkyrie.

She grinned, her teeth covered with sharpened gold caps. Her metallic wings shivered, their serrated edges nearly slicing the upholstery on my chair. "I grab the wand out of the chest and…"

Everyone held their breath.

"Throw it at the alien."

Everyone released their breath. We'd all assumed Flora was going to use the wand without any idea what sort of spells or curses it might hold or break it in half and release a nuclear blast of magical energy, or slip it in her pocket and make a run for it. A Valkyrie playing a human mage/thief didn't make for the most reliable member of our adventuring party.

Actually, none of them were very reliable when it came to teamwork.

My gaming buddies were a cyclops, a dragon, a Valkyrie, a pixie, a vampire, a nymph, and a dryad. Not the dryad that was our sheriff, but his sister. The woman was an absolute blast to play with and was trying to get her friend, a bunny shifter, to join the group. Evidently this bunny shifter lived outside the wards in the human world and in typical bunny shifter fashion, was nervous about venturing into a town with so many supernatural beings who might find her to be a delicious treat.

Of course we'd protect her, but that vow didn't do much to reassure a bunny shifter.

I rolled my percentile dice. "The wand bounces off the alien. Bob, you're up."

Bob was the vampire. Yep, *Bob*. Most vampires in town had elegant, old-world names, but Bob was Bob. I was pretty sure that wasn't his original name since he was roughly five hundred years old, but if that's what he wanted us to call him, then I was good with that.

"I pull my revolver and shoot." Bob rolled his dice and grimaced. "Eight."

"Yeah...no. Better luck aiming next time. Trapper?"

The pixie hovered above the table, his wings vibrating like a hummingbird's. "Spit."

I blinked. "Spit...…?"

"Spit, spit." He lowered himself to the table, eyeing his character sheet. "I've got that amulet of cobrafication from last year and I'm finally gonna use it."

Shit. I'd totally forgotten about that. Never doubt that a pixie would pull some crap out of a bag of holding from a campaign years ago and use it. They were worse than dragons when it came to hoarding.

I rolled my dice and sighed. "The spit hits. The alien howls and dark holes appear along his green-skinned chest. Ebony, you're next."

The dryad squirmed in her chair. "I swing my sword with all the might of my ginormous biceps. Did I mention I have ginormous biceps? And six-pack abs?"

John rolled his eyes…. eye. "Yes. Several times."

Ebony ignored him and rolled. "Twelve. Plus my bonuses."

"Miss." Everyone gasped at that, realizing how formidable their alien opponent truly was. "The alien opens his mouth and screams. The ground shakes, and everyone takes two points of damage and a negative one to their constitution."

There was a knock on the door, and I pushed back my chair. "Pizza's here. Let's take a break, and we'll resume once we all get a slice."

I headed for the door, hoping that it wasn't that poor blond guy that Lamira's Pizzeria seemed to send every week. Lamira's had the best wood-fired pizza, and they had the roasted red pepper topping that Trapper particularly enjoyed, but they were outside of the town wards and they were owned and operated solely by humans. Their delivery crew did include one coyote shifter, but for some reason he never got our orders. This poor blond human dude seemed to always be the unlucky guy who brought our pizza. Every time I opened the door and he got an eyeful of my friends, he'd freak out. I'd tip him big, and he'd practically throw the pizzas at me before racing for his car. As soon as he crossed the wards, he'd forget all about the pixie, Valkyrie, cyclops and other interesting beings in my living room, but I felt guilty about putting him through that every single week. Did repeated exposure to the magic of the wards do something to his brain? I really worried about that and probably should ask Bronwyn the next time I saw her.

I flung open the door, but instead of a human or a coyote shifter, the being at my doorway holding five pizza boxes was Eshu.

"You're working for Lamira's Pizzeria now?" I asked as I ushered him in.

"Nah. I saw the guy out front and figured I'd make the delivery for him."

My eyes narrowed with suspicion as he plopped the pizza boxes on my kitchen island and lifted the lids. "Please tell me you paid him. And tipped him."

"I'm told he won't remember it after crossing the wards," Eshu said with the most cheerful voice in the world.

I scowled and pulled out my phone, frantically making a payment on the app and adding in a tip. "Eshu, his boss will expect him to come back with cash. And tips are a major part of his income. That's not cool."

The demon-not-demon tilted his head, eyeing me with a puzzled expression.

"Here, Sylvie." Ebony handed me a ten. "This is my share."

The others also handed me cash, and I decided that it probably *was* a good idea to pay this all online and just have everyone chip in. Who knew what that poor delivery guy remembered after heading back out of town? I didn't want him getting in trouble because he couldn't remember how much we gave him or where the credit card copies were.

"Hey, man. I'm Fernando." The dragon reached out a beefy hand to shake Eshu's.

"Eshu. Sylvie is *my* couch-witch, so if any of you are planning on sleeping with her tonight, I'm letting you know you'll have to fight me first."

I felt my face heat up, but everyone in the room roared with laughter.

"Not like I haven't tried." Rio winked at me. Nymphs loved having sex with men, but it was women who they had lasting relationships with. And no, Rio had never hit on me. I was pretty sure I wasn't her type and that she was just messing with Eshu right now.

John laughed. "You do know she's a Perkins witch, right? She'll curse you to the ends of the earth if you screw her over. And if that's not enough, her sister will burn your pants off. That witch has got a fierce temper."

"Oh, stop." Bob shook his head. "This man, or whatever he is, should join our game. We could use someone new in the party. And, it's about time Sylvie had an admirer. She's pretty, for a witch."

Not the smoothest compliment I'd ever had, but I took it. "It's game night and sometimes we go to midnight," I told Eshu. "You're welcome to stay, or you could always come back after we're done."

Although I wasn't sure how energetic I'd be after we wrapped up. This was night three that Eshu had sought me out, and I hated to have this be night three that I was too tired to do more than fall asleep on the couch five minutes after he'd gotten here.

Eshu turned and the intensity of his gaze startled me. "I would enjoy staying, meeting your friends, and playing your game with you, but I don't want to interfere with your plans. If you would rather I come back, I will."

I felt as if something shifted between us. This wasn't just a booty call for him. He wanted to stay, hang out, game with us. I'd been assuming he was a total player and would want to keep what was between the two of us light and casual. Clearly, I'd been wrong.

It was up to me. Did I want things light and casual? I could tell him to come back later and set the terms for our relationship as friends with benefits, or I could ask him to stay and…what? Would that make him my boyfriend? Is that what I wanted?

"I can stand outside your door and wait for hours, maybe peering in the windows at you on occasion, just so I can catch a glimpse of your beauty," he said, still with that intense expression on his face that countered his teasing tone.

"That's weird, Eshu." I laughed. Then I made a decision. "Stay. Hang with us. Eat pizza. We've got white garlic with roasted red pepper, four-cheese deep dish, meat-meat-meat, mushroom/spinach/gorgonzola, and double anchovy. What would you like?"

"What's he eating?" Eshu looked over at Bob.

The vampire held up a go-cup with a lid. "Liquid diet."

"I'll do the double anchovy," Eshu said.

"Bold choice, my friend," I teased him. "Rio's the only one who normally likes the fish pizza."

The nymph shrugged. "What can I say? I've tried shrimp, crab meat, lobster, and salmon, but nothing beats anchovies. That salty brine…that little crunch…."

I shuddered but put a huge slice on a paper plate and handed it to the demon.

"Are you joining the game?" Trapper fluttered up near Eshu's face, barely keeping aloft with his giant slice of pizza in hand. "We're smack in the middle of a battle with an alien right now, but maybe you can play an NPC until Sylvie can bring you in."

"I can totally add you in that if you really want to play." I figured he was silly and quirky enough to enjoy this sort of thing and to fit in with my diverse bunch of players.

Eshu shrugged, taking a bite of the pizza. "Sure. I can play and stare at you adoringly all evening, imagining you naked and under me, and—"

"How about we stop at staring adoringly?" I interrupted

him. "I've got a bard side character that's about to join in, so you can play him if you want."

The demon nodded enthusiastically as he ate his slice of pizza.

We all walked back to my table. Eshu pulled a seat up next to me and did proceed to stare adoringly at me as we finished the battle with the alien. When we were done, Fernando's character was near death, but alive—which was a huge improvement over previous games. As the players searched the treasure chest further, they found a key, and at the back of the room, they found a cage with a man inside—a man who'd clearly not eaten well or bathed in a very long time.

"I let him out," Ebony announced.

"I hold my nose because he stinks," Trapper complained, actually pinching his nose.

"I see if he's fuckable," Rio said, eyeing Eshu as if she was in fact evaluating that very thing.

"You're playing a half-ogre warrior, Rio," I told her. "Not a nymph."

"Half-ogre warriors screw." She licked her lips. "And this half-ogre warrior likes what she sees."

I rolled my eyes then listened as the rest searched the room, patted down the dude in the cage, healed each other, and guarded the entrance. When they were done, I told them night was approaching and they all decided to make camp in that spot, setting up guard shifts and pulling a makeshift dinner from their packs. I'd slid Eshu a character sheet, which he'd glanced at briefly before scooting his chair closer to mine and putting his warm hand on my thigh. I tried to concentrate on the game, completely aware of his fingers massaging my leg through my pants, moving slowly upward into the danger zone.

"I see if any arrows or arrow heads are salvageable," John the Cyclops told me.

"I eat, then take first shift at guarding the entrance, but stay in the shadows so I'm not a target with the fire at my back," Flora the Valkyrie said.

"I put my belongings on the floor then lie on top of them so no one can steal them. Then I go to sleep," Fernando the dragon said.

"I'm going to sing," Eshu announced.

We all turned to stare at him. "What?" I asked.

"Sing." He shrugged. "It says on the paper I'm a bard, so I assume I'm supposed to sing all the time."

"Well, not all the time," I told him. "You sing as a profession. No one here is paying you. And you're malnourished and dirty. And you just got released from a cage where you've been kept by an alien for two weeks."

He shrugged. "Sounds like the perfect segue for a song to me."

Without further warning, he broke into an extremely bawdy, off-key ditty about a laundress and some crusaders, where the holy land was clearly a badly disguised metaphor for the woman's hoo-hoo. You could have heard a frickin' pin drop. And when he was done with the song, we stared at him for a moment, stunned. Then Bob, the vampire, applauded.

"I'm totally fucking this guy," Rio announced.

Something lit up inside me, fierce and full of a sense of ownership. I felt magic crackle around my skin a way I hadn't experienced for two weeks.

"You're not 'fucking' him," I told Rio in the sort of voice that would frost over hell itself.

Her eyebrows shot up and she raised her hands. "Okay. No problem, Sylvie. Not poaching at all. We nymphs know better than to do that. What's owned is owned."

"Sorry. If Sylvie isn't open to that sort of thing, then no can do," Eshu told the nymph. "I'm trying to get into this witch's pants, and it seems to be a full-time endeavor, so I doubt I'd have time for side hanky-panky either way."

"I've been through the crusades, and that's totally how it was," Bob declared, still fixated on Eshu's song. "Soldiers screwing their way through Europe on a papal-approved vacation. Don't get me wrong, I was thrilled. It was like a buffet on my doorstep. Actually, it was like one of those sushi places where the food goes by your table on little conveyor belts and you just grab what you want. I miss that."

Trapper rolled his eyes. "It's not like you have any problem getting blood. Or tail. Everyone gets horny over vampires. Everyone. Try being twelve inches."

Rio snickered. "I'll take that twelve inches, big boy."

"I'd suffocate," the pixie shot back. "I'm not a dildo with wings, you know."

"Can we keep playing?" Flora complained. "Not that this isn't an enlightening discussion or anything, but I'm guarding an entrance here and I want to know if anything is sneaking up on us, not about Bob and the crusades-buffet, or Trapper's size insecurity."

We got back to the game, Flora effectively alerting the party about a toxic creeping night slime, and Fernando and Eshu using fire to keep the slime away. At sunrise, the party moved on with Eshu's character in tow. In real life, it was ten o'clock at night. Normally we'd play on past midnight, but I was feeling tired, worried that I'd pushed myself too far so soon after my death and resurrection. So, I wrapped up, letting everyone know that I intended on continuing with the game next week. My friends collected their supplies, grabbing some pizza to go, and telling Eshu that they hoped he'd join our game on a permanent basis.

This sucked. The energy and libido I'd had earlier were

on a serious downslide. I'd been determined to take Eshu to bed the next time I saw him, but now that he was right here in my house, my heart and genitals were ready, but the rest of my body was thinking it was time to go to bed and actually sleep.

I wasn't supposed to have any more of Glenda's smoothie until tomorrow morning, but I made a split--second decision as my friends were leaving, pulling it out of the cabinet and taking a quick swig.

Ugh. It tasted horrible, but I did immediately feel more alert and awake. Putting it back in the cabinet, I shoved a mint into my mouth, hoping that it was enough to cover up the nasty breath I must have. It would really suck if Eshu went to kiss me and ran screaming because I tasted like moldy seaweed and old socks.

The demon had followed me into the kitchen, watching me as I drank the smoothie and popped the mint. He silently helped me clean up the empty pizza boxes, paper plates, and load the glasses in the dishwasher.

"Are you tired?" he asked, his hand sweeping down my back.

I nodded. "That was a healing potion in the jug, so I'm not quite as tired as I was a few minutes ago."

He wrapped his arms around my waist and pulled me against him, my back against his chest, his cheek against my hair. "Shall I carry you over to the couch and tuck you in?"

"No!" I held his hands on my stomach before he could scoop me up. "I don't need to sleep right now. I don't want to sleep right now."

I'd doze off and he'd leave, and while that did seem to be our thing, I wanted more tonight, and I definitely wanted to wake up with him beside me in my bed, not alone on the couch.

"Then what *do* you want, couch-witch?" he whispered in

my ear. "More games? Or should I pull out my giant trouser snake?"

Yes, please. Although a little romancing might be in order first.

"How about a drink?"

"I'm happy to accept an offering of alcohol," he informed me, planting a soft kiss on my neck before moving away to look in my cabinets for glasses.

I went to the fridge and pulled out a bottle of wine, holding it up and waiting for his thumbs-up before digging the corkscrew out of the drawer.

This had been a long day for a woman who'd died two weeks ago, but I felt oddly energized. Maybe it was the smoothie. Maybe it was the zing of having a gorgeous demon flirting with me and making it quite clear that he was one crook of my finger away from being in my bed.

Sexual tension. Even better than Glenda's smoothies. I'd need to remember that.

"What are these?"

I turned around to see Eshu holding up one of the charms I'd put together earlier today.

"I was trying to work some magic this afternoon, but I don't think I'm one hundred percent recovered yet," I admitted.

Funny how I could so easily tell him that, while I was hiding the same fact from Cassie.

"Understanding, affection, and calm. Yellow for creative solutions to a problem," he murmured, running his fingers over the buttons on the charm. I swear it felt as if he were touching me, stroking me with both his hands and his words.

I dragged in a ragged breath and tried to compose myself. "How did you know? Do you have experience with luck magic?"

He turned to me, and suddenly those dark eyes were so

full of intelligence, so serious that I blinked in surprise. "Indirectly, yes. But luck is your magic and I try to know everything I can about my couch-witch." He stroked the charm again and I stared, mesmerized, actually feeling his fingers as if they were on my skin.

"They're no good," I confessed. "Useless."

"Silly woman. They're beautifully constructed. You're a very talented witch."

"I *was* a very talented witch." I abandoned the wine bottle, walked over, and took the charm from his hands, placing it with the others on the counter.

"You still are a very talented witch. You're the best of all the witches. You're the best couch-witch ever to have walked the face of the earth."

I laughed. "I'm glad you think so, but that doesn't change the fact that these charms are nothing but a bunch of buttons on a string."

"They just need to be charged," he countered.

"And that's just what I can't do." I struggled to keep the bitterness from my voice. "I don't know if I can ever do that again. Maybe I'll craft the charms and have Cassie charge them, although they won't be the same as me doing it myself. I guess it's better than nothing."

He put his hands on my shoulders and pulled me toward him, kissing me with a thoroughness and a passion I hadn't expected. The moment his lips met mine, something thrummed through me. As the kiss deepened, it was like lightning in the room, bringing every cell in my body to attention, electricity igniting me. Fire roared through my body and I found myself wrapped around Eshu, trying to touch every bit of him, drinking in his kiss as if I had been in the desert for days.

When his mouth left mine, I was breathless, my weight against him as he kept me upright.

"You're not broken, my Sylvie," he whispered. "You're not dead or damaged. You just need to trust."

I had no idea who I was supposed to trust, but I felt like I was going to cry at his words. I wasn't broken? I wasn't damaged?

"I died, Eshu. I died and was resurrected because a reaper refused to cut the cord. Because a reaper loved my twin sister enough to shove my soul back into my body. What if...what if I'm not the same? What if some part of me that died never returned? I'm tired all the time. My magic is weak. I feel as if I'm walking every day through unfamiliar ground."

He smiled, his hands cupping my cheeks. "The last? The walking through unfamiliar ground thing? That's life, my couch-witch. The rest? It doesn't matter. None of that matters. You'll always be a witch. You'll always have magic. It might not be the same magic as before, but it will still be magic."

I gestured to the charms. "If I still have magic, then why are those useless? Why can't I power them?"

"Because your spark needs rekindling."

Was this a cheesy come-on? Was this where he told me that sex with him would bring my power back? I knew that demons accentuated both Cassie's and Bronwyn's powers, but those were demons who they'd bonded with. I doubted sex with Eshu would do the same.

Although I was willing to give it a try, because right now sex with Eshu was at the top of my to-do list.

"Here." He turned and picked up the charms, dumping them in my hands. "Just feel your magic and let it fly."

I closed my eyes and held the button charms gently. My fingers smoothed along the plastic edges, felt the woolen thread that held the buttons together, felt the shape and size and the holes of the charms. I pictured their colors in my mind, thought of understanding, affection, and calm, of creative and innovative solutions to problems.

I felt Eshu's hands on mine. I felt his fingers caressing my knuckles. I felt the heat of him near me, the caress of his breath on my cheek. Once again, his energy soared through me. He kissed my neck and I shivered, trying to concentrate on the charms and failing. Everything faded away except the feel of his lips against my skin, and the surge of his energy lighting me up inside. It was like a rush of electricity, like lightning, like dying and being reborn into something timeless.

Like the ebb of the tide, I felt Eshu's power begin to slide away. The golden glow dimmed, and once again I was aware of the charms in my hands, of my legs that trembled so hard I could barely stand, of the press of the demon's body behind me, of the dampness between my thighs.

Of the hard length of him pressed against my rear end.

Snatching the last bit of energy before it left me, I pushed it into the charms, thrilled to feel them heat in my hands. It left me feeling tired and drained, desperately in need of sleep. But there was something else I needed far more right now.

Sitting the charms on the counter, I turned around and wrapped my arms around Eshu's neck, my eyes meeting his.

"Thank you," I murmured, placing a soft kiss on his lips.

"What I have is yours, my couch-witch," he murmured back. "But that wine you offered before will be a sufficient expression of gratitude."

"How about I offer you something else instead?"

I kissed him again, but this time he gripped me tight, rubbing his hips against mine and refusing to let me pull away. I gasped, and he took advantage, his tongue exploring my mouth as his hands did the same with my body. I yanked the shirt from his pants and fumbled with his belt, making a frustrated noise when I couldn't manage to get the darned thing to unbuckle.

He wasn't having the same problem. While I was smashing my fingers trying to get his belt undone, he'd already pushed my shirt up, unhooked my bra, and managed to get my pants down to my knees. I pulled my mouth from his, thinking I might have to grab a knife from the butcher block to cut the darned belt off him and lost my balance, nearly falling to the floor.

Eshu grabbed me, lifting me up to slide my pants off, then setting me back down to practically dislocate my shoulders trying to pull my shirt over my head.

"Hey! Slow down a minute," I complained. "This isn't a race. And I haven't even gotten your stupid belt off yet."

He stepped back, leaving me in my underwear with a shirt halfway off my shoulders and my bra hanging loose from my arms. I shrugged out of the shirt and bra before eyeing the demon before me.

"Hold still," I commanded before slowly unbuttoning his shirt and sliding it off him, taking a moment to appreciate what I'd just revealed. Dark skin gleamed across lean muscles that begged to be tasted. I traced a line from his collarbone down to his pants, once more trying in vain to remove his belt.

Screw it. With a quick motion, I pulled a knife from the butcher block, slid it between the leather and fabric and sliced through the belt with one quick motion. Eshu sucked in a quick breath and I looked up to see him watching me with alarm.

"That…that was both erotic and terrifying, couch-witch. I thought for a moment there I was going to die again, and that it would not be a particularly pleasant death."

I spun the knife around in my hand then turned to put it

back in the butcher block. "I'm a luck witch, remember. You had nothing to fear."

"Luck is a tricky thing. One person's luck is another's curse." He reached down and felt his crotch. "It's still there. It's still hard. If you're done slicing things off my body with sharp knives, then let's move this to your couch."

I reached down and unfastened his pants, thankful that I didn't have the same problem with them as I'd had with the belt. "Let's go to my bed instead of the couch," I told him.

He grinned, stepping forward to scoop me up into his arms. "As you command, my bed-witch. As you command."

CHAPTER 11

SYLVIE

*J*ran, barely making it to my office before nine o'clock and thinking the whole way that Eshu was a very bad influence on me.

The other two nights when he'd tucked me to sleep on the couch, he'd been gone by the time I'd awakened in the morning. That had been my fear—that I'd wake to an empty bed, and that after having sex with him throughout the night, he'd vanish, and I'd never see him again. Instead, I slowly came to a drowsy consciousness to find him spooning me, his one leg wrapped around mine, his arm around my waist. I stirred. He stirred. Then we had that lovely half-asleep morning sex that is truly the best way to start the day.

We made cheese omelets in the nude, ate in the nude, then went back to bed for some post-breakfast seduction. I barely had time for a quick shower and had to leave with my hair wet and no makeup on. I was almost late for the nine o'clock appointment I'd set up, and that would have been horribly unprofessional of me.

Breakfast. Drat. I'd promised Bart pastries or something like that. I didn't have time to race over to the bakery before they arrived, so I decided that would be my excuse to leave them alone to talk together.

Unlocking the door, I got to work putting on a pot of coffee and firing up the kettle. Stanley arrived first, right at nine o'clock. I made him his favorite tea and tried to look busy while he sat and fidgeted, looking over to the door every ten seconds. Finally, I sat down and tried to take his mind off things by discussing a knocking sound my car was making and asking him to troubleshoot the problem.

Fifteen minutes after the hour, I started to worry. Was he not coming? Had Bart knuckled under to the fear that the pack might find out if he disobeyed the exile mandate, deciding his friendship with Stanley wasn't worth the risk? Had I made things with Stanley worse, getting his hopes up like this only to have him experience the equivalent of being ditched on prom night with his dress on and hair done?

It was twenty after, and I had pretty much sweated through my anti-perspirant and was completely out of small talk when Stanley sat up in his chair, his shoulders straightening and an excited expression flitting across his face. Two minutes later, Bart edged through my door, his eyes darting everywhere as if he expected either a surprise party or Dallas to jump out and bite him.

"Come in. Grab some coffee or some tea and sit down," I told him. "I was running a bit late today, but once you guys get settled in, I can dash out and grab some pastries."

"I'm good. Ate a big breakfast," Bart said as he walked over and poured some coffee into a mug. He didn't look at Stanley. Stanley didn't look at him.

Great. We were off to such a wonderful start here.

"So…" I waited until the pair were seated. Bart had taken the chair at an angle from Stanley on the couch. Not too close, but not across the room, either. "Let's start with Bart. What's been going on in your life the past few weeks?"

The werewolf slid Stanley a glance out of the corner of his eyes. "I can't discuss pack matters in front of...you know."

I got a horrible feeling this wasn't going to go well. Stanley would be even more despondent, and I would have totally screwed up any small progress he'd made toward his being happy as a lone wolf. Was it just my powers that were gone? Maybe my abilities as a therapist had taken a hit with my death as well.

Taking a calming breath, I decided to keep going with this. They were both here in the same room. That had to be indicative of some interest on Bart's part to keep in contact with Stanley against Dallas's mandate.

"Then let's not talk about pack politics or any of that. We'll discuss personal stuff instead."

Bart looked down at his coffee cup. "Went fishing Tuesday. Caught a bass and threw it on the smoker."

Stanley grunted. "How big?"

Bart shrugged. "Twelve? Thirteen inches?"

"You got him at the bend? With the downed tree?" There was a pained note in Stanley's voice that made me think they had caught a lot of fish together at this spot.

"Yeah." Bart shifted in his seat, facing Stanley but still not looking at him. "Been out there a few times but only caught the one."

Stanley nodded knowingly. "You use golden shiners?"

Bart snorted. "You keep your shiners. Crawfish are better bait for bass."

I had no idea what these guys were talking about but having gotten the conversation started, I quietly excused myself and ran down to the bakery. By the time I got back with a box of cream-filled donuts, the two were sprawled on the couch watching Ice Road Truckers on the television. They dug into the donuts, and I made myself busy with some paperwork, noting that aside from the occasional commentary about the foolhardiness of the truckers on TV, they were completely silent.

It was a good silence, a companionable silence. When the show was over, Bart stood, saying that he needed to get going. Stanley stood as well, saying he hoped to see him next week, and that he'd bring that three-eighths inch socket wrench Bart wanted to borrow.

Bart grunted in appreciation, his eyes meeting the other werewolf's for the first time. "Thanks. I'll smoke some ribs."

Ribs? At nine on Sunday? I withheld judgement because Stanley seemed excited about the prospect. Bart left, holding his amulet tightly and looking carefully around before venturing through the doorway and outside. Stanley waited another ten minutes, then took out his own amulet, turning to me before he left.

"Thanks, Sylvie."

He walked out and I felt downright giddy with happiness. It had been a success. Maybe they couldn't hunt—or fish—together yet, but at least Stanley had been able to have contact with another werewolf—one who he counted as his friend. I could tell by the man's posture and the ease in his face that he felt better. He was less depressed, calmer, and content.

It wasn't a long-term solution but for twelve weeks of "tap dance lessons," Bart and Stanley would be able to get together and talk...or watch television, or do whatever guys did to bond. Maybe I could figure out a way for them to meet outside my office, if I could manage to get my magic to the point where I could make some additional amulets keyed to a different location.

Either way, I felt good about today. I'd made a difference in a werewolf's life. Hopefully the meeting Monday would go just as well, and we'd be even closer to peace among the werewolves and a happy life for all of them.

CHAPTER 12

SYLVIE

$\mathcal{I}$ drove over to Cassie's, filled with that warm contentedness that suffused me every Sunday when we all got together for dinner. We might all be adults with our own homes, careers, and lives, but I loved how we connected as a group every week. Seven sisters and Aaron, our cousin who we treated as a brother, shared dinner and talked about our lives, reconnecting and reaffirming our connection with each other. There were occasions when Ophelia was working at the firehouse and couldn't make it, and those Sundays always felt a bit empty. We made sure to bring her leftovers, but still missed her presence—me, especially.

But in the past few months, family dinners had become different. First there was Lucien, and I'd be the first to admit it had been an adjustment having him suddenly in the midst of what for all of us was a sacred event. A demon. A stranger. Some hot guy that Cassie was leading around by the nose and was a bit infatuated with. We'd never allowed boyfriends at Sunday dinner. We'd never allowed friends. Even when Cassie had been dating Marcus, and they'd been fairly serious at one point, he'd never been allowed to invade the sanctity of Sunday Family Dinner. Yet in less than a week of his appearance, Lucien was there, breaking bread with us as if he were family.

I wasn't the only sister that had problems with his sudden inclusion, but I was the only sister who'd confronted Cassie about it. We'd had an emotion-laden, but productive conversation, and in the end, I'd realized that although their relationship seemed inexplicably sudden to me, it was a deep and forever connection as far as Cassie was concerned.

Just as I had lectured her about treating me like an adult and respecting my judgement on when I felt able to return to work and go back home, she'd done the same with me about her relationship with Lucien. Respect went two ways, and during our conversation, I'd realized I needed to accept what Cassie and my other sisters might call a significant relationship—one significant enough that the "other" should be considered family and included in our weekly dinners.

Lucien had been savvy enough to ease his way into the family. He'd been friendly and polite, sitting quietly during conversation until he felt welcome enough to contribute. He'd paved the way, and when Bronwyn had brought Hadur in, we'd welcomed him with open arms. Of course, part of that was because he'd rescued her from her wrecked truck and taken care of her. And Bronwyn, was...Bronwyn. She was feisty and funny, and she didn't trust easily. The warm glow in her expression when she'd looked at Hadur had told us all we needed to know. If Bronwyn wanted to bring a warmonger to our family night dinner, then we'd eagerly accept him.

And Nash had been an easy-yes as well. He'd resurrected me when I'd died. And it was clear to anyone with eyes in their head that he adored Ophelia. Plus, Nash had the sort of calm, kind, gentle personality that made him welcome anywhere. Who would have thought a reaper could be so agreeable?

Three demons. Well, two demons and a reaper. It was a good thing Cassie had a giant dining room table that could accommodate our growing family.

Cassie was in the kitchen, kneading a huge quantity of ground beef in a big stainless-steel bowl. Beside her, Adrienne stood peeling potatoes and dropping them into a pot.

"I'm here early," I announced. "What do you need me to do?"

"Addy could use some help with the potatoes," Cassie instructed. "But first hand me that can of tomato sauce, please."

Meatloaf. Most of us would have bought some pre-prepared stuff from the grocery store and shoved it in the oven, but Cassie was old enough to remember making meatloaf with our grandmother and she knew the recipe. Ground beef. Eggs. Spices. Tomato sauce. Onions. Peppers. And rice for some inexplicable reason. It was super tasty, and every bite reminded me of home and family.

"Can you open that second one so I can pour it over the top?" Cassie asked me.

I used the old-fashioned hand-cranked can opener, handed it to her, then put the eggs back in the fridge before joining Adrienne at the sink. Lucien came in before I'd gotten more than one potato peeled, walking over and giving Cassie a kiss that had Adrienne telling the pair of them to get a room.

"Thought you were going to miss tonight's dinner," I said to the demon. "Cassie mentioned there was some trouble in hell you were dealing with."

Lucien made a growling noise and threw his hands upward. "I'm ready to blast the whole third circle into nothingness. What a bunch of boneheads."

"If you do that, will there just be a hole in hell?" Adrienne asked.

"A hell-hole," I teased.

Adrienne grinned. "Or maybe it would be a spot you need to jump over, where you tell the newly arrived 'oh, that used to be the third circle, but we had to nuke it because they were dicks'?"

Cassie laughed. "Or like the thirteenth floor in some buildings? Hell will just skip from the second circle to the fourth, and if people ask about the third circle, you just shudder and tell them 'it's bad luck to have a third circle'?"

"Or maybe just name it something else, like circle two-and-a-half," I joked. "'We don't talk about the third circle, man. Nobody talks about the third circle.'"

"What's going on anyway?" Adrienne asked. "I thought you guys had a pretty tight grip on things down there?"

"Instructions for the third circle went to the fifth instead, and a message that was supposed to be delivered two weeks ago just now got there." Lucien shook his head. "Basically, Eshu screwed up, which he seems to do a lot."

I hid a wince at Eshu's name, bending my head to concentrate on the potatoes.

"So fire him," Adrienne told him.

"I can't." Lucien shrugged. "No one can. He's the only one who can be in both hell and heaven. He can go anywhere, talk to anyone. He doesn't technically report to us, so there's nothing we can do except complain about him—which does absolutely nothing."

"I thought he was a demon?" Cassie looked at Lucien in surprise. "I thought he was a demon or an angel who had some sort of diplomatic immunity?"

Lucien wobbled his hand back and forth. "Technically, he's neither. We're the same—angels and demons. It's just who we report to, our duties, and some after-the-fact traits that make us a tiny bit different. Eshu's kind of like us, but not. And during the split when my father told my grandfather to get bent and headed out on his own, Eshu didn't take sides."

"So he's Switzerland," Adrienne commented.

"If you mean a frivolous, silly, slacker Switzerland, then yes." Lucien shook his head. "Eshu was different even before the split. He's really old. I think he might even be older than my grandfather."

"He doesn't seem that old," I mused.

"That's because he never really grew up," Lucien said. "We can't fire him. We can't punish him. All we can do is yell at him, which doesn't seem to make one bit of difference. And we need him. He's the messenger."

The messenger. The communicator. The one who walked freely between heaven and hell and the mortal realm. Who was this demon-not-a-demon? I'd caught a glimpse of someone brilliant and powerful and wise for a moment in my kitchen last night before he'd returned to his playful, chaotic self. Which was the real Eshu?

Perhaps both were the real Eshu.

All I knew was that I'd been sad to return home from my office to find him gone. He'd found my stash of mini peanut butter cups and ate them all, leaving the wrappers on the counter with a note thanking me. I wasn't sure if the thanks was for the candy, or the sex, or maybe both, but the house felt empty and quiet without him there. It felt less alive. *I* felt less alive.

"We're here!" Bronwyn shouted from the living room.

Next thing I knew, the kitchen was jam packed with people. Bronwyn and Hadur had brought a couple of pies for dessert. Aaron was carrying what looked like a case of wine. Babylon had a salad in her hands, and Glenda had a bag with French bread sticking out of the top. Ophelia and Nash brought up the rear, squeezing into the tiny space and offering to help.

"Here. I've got this." Nash took the peeler from my hands with a smile. "I've been prepping potatoes all week at the diner, so I'm a bit of an expert. You and your sisters go relax. Get started on Aaron's wine."

Aaron held up a bottle in one hand, flipping a corkscrew in the other as if he were a ninja. "Nash is right. Let the guys cook for once. You gals into the living room."

"I'm not leaving my meatloaf in non-Perkins hands," Cassie announced. "Let me get it in the oven, then you men can take over."

Bronwyn, Adrienne, Babylon, and Ophelia headed out while Glenda and I started pulling wine glasses from the cabinet.

"Your aura looks amazing," Glenda whispered to me. "What did you do?"

I shot her a puzzled look. "Drank your smoothies? Moved off Cassie's couch and back into my own house? Went back to work? Ate pizza and had game night?"

"As much as I'd like to claim credit, that aura isn't from my smoothies. And I doubt it's pizza." She hesitated, a fistful of glasses in each hand. "It's...red. Red and black, but the black isn't a bad sort of black. It's shiny, glossy, reflective. I've never seen you this powerful."

"Why thank you." I simpered and curtsied, but Glenda's compliments gave me a surge of hope that things might actually go well tomorrow at the meeting. The luck charms were charged, and if my aura really was so outstanding, then maybe I could start off the week by getting the werewolves to come to a peaceful, mutually beneficial agreement.

"Powerful, but...unstable."

Crap. I didn't like the sound of that one bit.

"Be careful, Sylvie. I don't know what's going on, and I'm

no oracle, but I think whatever you do might end up having unexpected results."

Yeah. I really didn't like the sound of that. Turning around to grab two opened wine bottles from Aaron, I was shocked to see Eshu walk into the kitchen.

"Something smells amazing!" His voice was cheerful, and he rubbed his hands together in anticipation. Crazy demon. There wasn't anything to smell yet. Cassie hadn't even put the meatloaf into the oven.

"And wine! Is this for me?" He took a bottle from Aaron, then reached out to boop me on the nose. "You, I will share with. I share my offerings with no one but you, couch-witch."

"You've got to be kidding me," Lucien snapped. "It's Sunday. It's supposed to be my day off. This better be urgent if someone is sending me a message during family dinner night."

"I've got no message for you, son of Satan. I'm here for dinner and this freely given offering of wine. Is that meatloaf? I love meatloaf!" Eshu walked over to where Cassie was forming the loaf. She glared, putting herself between our dinner and the demon.

"Lucien? Are you inviting your co-workers to Sunday family dinner? Because I have a problem with that."

Lucien's eyes widened and he raised his hands. "No! I would never do that, Cassie. Eshu…just shows up some-times." He turned to the other demon. "Get out of here. Go to hell, or to heaven, or New York or something, but get out of our house."

Eshu tried to peer around Cassie's shoulder at the meat-loaf. "I go wherever I will. There is no place forbidden to me, no rule I must follow, no law that compels me to abide."

"Oh, you are going to follow my rules, or else," Cassie snapped. "Lucien? Get him out of here or I will."

Fire sparked on Cassie's fingers. Lucien's eyes turned coal

black. Eshu ignored all the warning signs and kept trying to look at the meatloaf over Cassie's shoulder. I threw up my hands and dove between them all, shielding the silly not-demon from their wrath.

"Whoa, whoa. Family dinner night. It's the one time we get together to relax and not incinerate uninvited guests." I pointed to Cassie as she was clearly the angrier of the two. "Put the meatloaf in the oven. I'll...I'll talk to Eshu and straighten this out."

My sister blinked, the fire abruptly extinguishing from her fingertips. Then she tilted her head as she regarded me. "Sylvie, you're always the peacemaker, but just let me handle this one."

I waved her off, pushing Eshu backward from the kitchen. "Nope. You're in charge of meatloaf. The guys are handling the rest of the dinner. I've got this."

Before she could reply, I had Eshu out of the kitchen and into the dining room. My other sisters peered at me in surprise. I ignored their curious stares as I wrestled the bottle of wine from Eshu's hands, putting it on the table before shoving him toward the tiny half-bathroom beside the staircase.

"That wine is an offering to me," Eshu complained. "It's mine. No one better touch it. Except for you, couch-witch. You are welcome to all my offerings. And my giant cock. You're always welcome to that."

I looked heavenward, shaking my head as I pushed him into the bathroom and shut the door behind me.

"What are you doing here?" I hissed, poking him in the chest. Cassie and Lucien had heard Eshu proposition me for the two weeks I'd recovered on the couch, but none of my other sisters had and I was pretty sure they were all dying of curiosity on the other side of this door.

Well, except for Ophelia, that is.

"It's family dinner night." He pulled me into his arms and kissed me.

I'll admit for a split second I forgot about the awkwardness of having my casual fling show up for family dinner night and wondered if said family would notice my absence for ten or fifteen minutes. Maybe twenty minutes. How fast could we do it, and what positions would we manage in this tiny powder-room?

I put a hand on his chest and reluctantly pulled away. "Eshu, it's *family* dinner night. *Family*."

"I know. And it's meatloaf. I love meatloaf." He tried to kiss me again and I did my best to evade him.

"We're not...you're not." I grimaced, wondering how the heck I was going to say this without hurting his feelings or sounding like a callous witch. "Eshu, we're friends. We've slept together once. That's not a family-dinner level relationship."

"Not once, eight times." He'd given up and instead was now trailing kisses down my neck, pulling me tight against his rather impressive erection. "Unless you're talking actual sleep. In that case, I'm not sure if the few hours we got here and there even qualifies as once. I'd like to sleep with you though, my couch-witch. After lots of sex, that is."

I was seriously ready to throw caution to the winds and screw this guy in the bathroom. The meatloaf and my family could wait. I wavered, then firmed up my resolve.

"Eshu, lots of sex in a twenty-four-hour period does not mean you get to just show up at family dinner. You're not family."

"Lucien, Hadur, and Nash aren't family," he argued, still kissing my neck. "And neither is that raccoon hanging out by the back door that your one sister slips food to throughout the evening."

"They're in a long-term relationship with my sisters," I

argued back. "Well, except for the raccoon, and as you'll notice, he's not inside with a plate set at the table. You and I don't have a long-term relationship. We're friends who had a whole lot of sex last night and this morning."

"I think that qualifies." He pulled back, his dark eyes searching mine. "But if you don't want me here, if you are embarrassed by what we have with each other and don't want your family to know. If you want me to go, then I will."

I felt like a total jerk at his words. And it was true—I *was* a bit ashamed of what we had together. I was having a hot-and-heavy casual sex thing with a not-quite-a-demon that Cassie and Lucien disapproved of. If I were my own client, I'd be having a serious discussion right now about my need for my eldest sister's approval, and why I felt it was important for me to hold on to a false persona of not being the sort of woman who brought a silly, frivolous demon into her home and had no-strings-attached sex with him *all night long*.

I saw the hurt in his eyes, but I also saw a devilish gleam there and had been a therapist long enough to know what that meant.

"Eshu, emotional manipulation does not establish a good foundation for a relationship. If you truly want something going forward with me, whether that's a friends-with-benefits deal or something more, then you need to be honest and open with your emotions."

He grinned and rubbed himself against me. "My couch-witch is brilliant. And beautiful. And sexy. I love meatloaf. I want to stay and be part of your family and enjoy Sunday dinners with you all. But if you truly think it's best for me to leave, then I will. I only ask that you slip me a plate of meatloaf and mashed potatoes out the back door like your sister does with the raccoon."

I burst out laughing, something warm and electric sparking inside of me. I lov—liked this guy. I liked him a lot.

Screw it. We'd never allowed casual boyfriends at Sunday night dinner, but Lucien, Hadur, and Nash hadn't exactly been with my sisters very long before they started attending. Technically Nash attended uninvited that first night when he appeared to take my soul and ended up resurrecting me.

I was making a judgement call. And if anyone had a problem with it, they could address it with me tomorrow, after we'd enjoyed meatloaf.

"I'll set a place for you at the table." I snaked my hands around Eshu's neck. "Can't have you eating outside with the raccoon, can I?"

He caught his breath, then slid his hands down to my ass, lifting me off my feet and against him as his lips claimed mine. My legs wrapped around his hips, pushing hard against him as he spun me around, then took a step forward and pressed my back against the narrow wall. My fingers stroked his neck as he held my rear with one hand and snaked the other up the front of my shirt.

There was a bang on the door, and I shrieked into his mouth, letting go of Eshu's neck. Thankfully, he seemed unbothered by the interruption as he continued to hold me upright and against the wall, fondling me through my bra, his tongue dancing with mine.

"Sylvie?" Glenda called out. "Are you guys done in there? I've got to pee, and I don't want to have to go all the way upstairs. Heaven knows what sorts of kinky stuff Cassie is keeping in that bathroom."

I broke off our kiss, resting my forehead against Eshu's shoulder while I tried to catch my breath. It wasn't easy since he was completely ignoring Glenda and still caressing my boobs.

"Just…just a second," I called out. Then I pushed Eshu's hand out of my shirt, tugging the hem down as I lowered my legs to the floor.

"She doesn't have to pee that bad," Eshu told me, trying once more to hike my legs up.

I swatted his hands away. "Stop. Later. At my house, after dinner."

"Eight times?" He bent down and nibbled my ear.

"Twelve," I promised him.

"Sylvie?" Glenda banged on the door again.

"Coming!" I shouted.

"I wish," Eshu muttered.

I pushed around him, opening the door and giving Glenda a weak smile. "Done. It's all yours," I told her.

"We were *not* done," Eshu announced. "You could have held your urine for quite a bit longer."

Glenda's eyebrows went up and she bit back a smile. "So...I take it this demon is staying for dinner?"

I sucked in a breath, ready to tell her that yes, Eshu was staying, and that it wasn't anyone's business what we were doing in our free time as I was an adult who was almost thirty and perfectly capable of deciding what relationships I wanted to have with whom.

"Good." Glenda chuckled. "I like him. I think we need him in this family."

Eshu puffed his chest out at her words.

"He's...we're just friends," I sputtered.

Glenda nodded knowingly. "Well, your aura says otherwise. Now get out of this bathroom so I can pee."

CHAPTER 13

ESHU

*I*f some demon had told me three weeks ago that I'd be following a witch around, tucking her in at night, participating in role playing games not of the sexual kind, and freely giving her my energy to power her charms, I would have thought he'd been hitting the nectar of the gods a bit too hard.

As for crashing her family-night dinner...well, I didn't lie when I said I loved meatloaf. But no meatloaf in the world would have been sufficient for me to willingly spend hours with that annoying spawn of Satan glowering at me. No, I was there for Sylvie, because I missed her every moment I wasn't with her. I missed her laugh. I missed her quick mind. Something fun and interesting would happen to me, and all I could think about was how much more fun and interesting it would have been had my couch-witch been there to share the experience.

I wasn't truly a demon and not truly an angel, but I still bonded like they did, and I could feel myself bonding to this witch. And I had absolutely no interest at all in fighting it.

So, I threw myself into the event that was family-dinner

night. I got to know her sisters and her sisters' lovers. That eldest sister was a bossy stick-in-the-mud, but the rest of them were quite amusing. None of the others had ever died, let alone died by microwaving hot fudge, but they were still reasonably entertaining.

I tried to be on my best behavior, but to be honest, I had no idea how to behave around demons and angels, let alone a bunch of witches. Who knew that drinking games were not appropriate at family-night dinner? Or that I wasn't supposed to tell that story about Lucien and the beholder? Or accidently drop mashed potatoes into Lucien's lap. Okay, so it wasn't an accident, and I didn't exactly "drop" the mashed potatoes, nor did they go into his lap. Truthfully, I flung them into his face from my spoon.

Evidently food fights were not appropriate at family-night dinner. I also discovered that the racoon was not supposed to come inside to eat pie with the rest of us. Although I had a wonderful time watching everyone chase the animal around the room, a few attendees weren't amused.

Sylvie was amused, especially when the racoon swiped the can of whipped cream and somehow managed to get on top of the light fixture with it. Racoons like whipped cream. I didn't blame the guy; I liked whipped cream as well, especially if I got to lick it off my beloved witch.

After the racoon was banished outside, and Sylvie made a convincing argument for why *I* shouldn't be banished outside, the cleanup commenced. I remained in the living room area with the others while the eldest sister and one of the younger ones dragged my Sylvie into the kitchen to do dishes and "talk."

"I like seeing her laugh again," Sylvie's twin sister told me. "You make her happy."

"I want to make her happy," I replied.

The twin gave me a searching look. "Don't hurt her, okay? She's been through a lot. She died and Nash resurrected her. She's still healing and trying to figure out how to deal with the aftermath of what happened. Just don't hurt her."

I would never hurt my couch-witch.

"She told me about her death." I gave the twin a knowing nod. "A microwave and hot fudge. That's incredibly impressive. And creative. I'm glad your reaper assisted her, because I would have hated for her to be dead-dead. Of course, I never would have met her if she hadn't died and needed to convalesce on her sister's couch,. I owed your reaper my gratitude. And the microwave that electrocuted her as well."

The twin shot me a strange look. "Do you love her?"

Did I? I'd only known her a few weeks, but I was fairly certain I did love her.

"I've had sex with many men and women in my life, yet none has ever captivated me like Sylvie," I confessed.

She wasn't like the others. It wasn't just sex that the couch-witch wanted from me. It's not like she wanted me to do magic for her or grant her favors or intervene with some powerful being on her behalf. She hadn't even made an offering to me, which normally would have been a deal breaker in any relationship.

She liked *me*. She enjoyed my company as much as she enjoyed my staff of love. She liked *me*. And when I made her laugh, it was the best feeling in the world—even better than sex.

Okay, that was a lie, but it was close to sex. Very close.

How could I win her over, get her to care about me the same way I did about her? How could I make her see me as worthy of being a part of her family, of being her one-and-only? I thought about the few weeks I'd known her, and suddenly knew what I had to do. It would be the perfect gift.

I would help her by not helping her, then helping her. Yes. That would be the best gift ever. And maybe then she'd fall in love with me just as I was falling in love with her.

CHAPTER 14

SYLVIE

"You're not seriously sleeping with him?" Cassie hissed. She was washing dishes with Adrienne drying as I scooped leftovers into containers.

"Do you want the details? Because, wow, my life is pretty much like a porno right now."

Cassie shuddered. "No, I most definitely don't want the details."

"I do," Adrienne chimed in.

Screw it. The moment I'd made the decision to let Eshu stay for dinner, I knew that there was no way I could play this off as just friends. My sisters believed I was kinky as all get out. I specialized in relationship counselling dealing with sex issues, and I loved to shock them by recommending specific sex toys or positions. My boinking someone casually shouldn't come as a shock to any of them.

But it did come as a shock. For all my talk, I'd never been one for partying it up or promiscuous behavior. The fact that it was Eshu probably bothered Cassie the most. I knew she didn't see the attraction.

And *that* bothered me. Lucien, Hadur, and Nash didn't

128

appeal to me beyond my acknowledging they were good-looking dudes, but I didn't doubt how my sisters could be attracted to—or in love with—them. Not that I was in love with Eshu or anything, but why couldn't Cassie see how he was fun, exciting, and sexy? How he made me laugh so hard I felt like I was going to pee my pants? How sex with him was a wild, uninhibited ride?

"Chill out, Cass," Adrienne scolded. "I'd do him. Damn, the shoulders on that guy... And I'll bet he's got some serious moves."

"He does," I assured her. "I barely got any sleep last night, and I'm doubting I'll get any tonight, either."

"No details!" Cassie turned to me, drying off her soapy hands. "Sylvie, you're a grown woman and who you're sleeping with isn't any business of mine, but why Eshu? He's such a screw up. He's not smart. Lucien hates him. He doesn't seem your type at all."

I wasn't sure what to address in all that first. "Lucien hates Hadur as well, and you're not telling Bronwyn to leave him home."

"Hadur saved Bronwyn's life," Cassie shot back.

"That's not the point," Adrienne chimed in. "Lucien's your boyfriend. He's not family. His likes and dislikes carry no weight on whether Sylvie gets to bring Eshu to family dinner."

"Secondly," I continued, silently grateful for Adrienne's support, "I don't really have a 'type.' I like men whose company I enjoy and those who I'm physically attracted to. That encompasses a wide range of men. He might not be *your* type, but he makes me laugh and he's incredible in the sack."

"And he's not stupid," Adrienne added. "I think he acts like that to piss Lucien off."

I got the impression Eshu loved to throw people off

balance, to have people underestimate him, to operate under the radar. It didn't matter to him that everyone else thought he was dumb and a screw up. All that mattered was enjoying life and being a living personification of the id.

And as a therapist, I appreciated the value of that—especially in my own personal life.

"Is he your boyfriend?" Cassie took me by the shoulders, her eyes on mine. "Is he? If you care about him and think this is something that's going to last, then I'll back you one hundred percent, Sylvie. He'll be welcome here in our house, and I'll tell Lucien to just deal. But I need to know what's between you guys is real and not you just having a wild fling because you almost died two weeks ago."

I hesitated because I didn't really know how to answer that question. And it was a bit unfair of Cassie to ask me this. Had she known Lucien was going to be a long-term thing when she'd first met him?

"All I know is that right now, I don't want to date or sleep with anyone else. I'm happy with him. Am I going to feel that way in two months or two years or two decades? I don't know. I only know that for now, you all should consider him my boyfriend."

It scared me a bit to say that. Two weeks he'd flirted with me while I'd recovered on Cassie's couch, and I'd thought that was as far as things would go between us. Two nights of what I'd consider dating. One night of intimacy. It seemed kind of fast to label that an actual relationship, but here I was doing just that.

"Good enough for me," Adrienne said, folding the dish towel and hanging it on the oven handle.

Cassie sighed. "Good enough for me, too."

"And Lucien?" I asked.

She laughed. "He got used to Hadur. He's going to have to get used to Eshu as well."

With the most difficult topic of the evening out of the way, I attempted to broach the other one. "About tomorrow night...."

Adrienne's eyebrows shot up. "What about tomorrow night?"

Cassie sighed. "I meant what I said before. I spoke to Sheriff Oakes about Stanley, and he's going to put a deputy out there. I also told Lucien that I want us to go over just before midnight, because that's when everyone likes to do whatever it is they plan on doing. He'll be safe. I give you my word on that."

"And the attack on Clinton's pack?" I asked.

"Unless Clinton asks for our protection, I don't know what we can do about that," Cassie replied.

Adrienne snorted. "Like he'd ask for our protection. Maybe if there were meteors raining from the sky, or an alien attack, or a volcano coming up in the middle of their mountain. He's the alpha of his pack. He's not going to ask for protection from his own father."

"I'm going to go up there, then." I wasn't sure what the heck I was going to do, but maybe I could make a difference. If I took Eshu with me, perhaps I could use his power again and hex anyone who threatened Clinton's pack. He'd helped me power the luck charms; I was pretty sure I could convince him to help me with this project as well.

"No." Cassie slapped a hand on the counter. "I'm not having you smack in between two groups of fighting werewolves."

"I'll go with her," Adrienne interjected. "There's seven of us, Cassie. If you're going to be head witch and run Accident, then you need us to help. There's too much for one witch to do, even one as powerful as you are."

"You and Lucien protect Stanley," I told Cassie. That was of primary importance. The lone wolves were counting on us to protect them, and if something happened, all of Accident would question our ability to stand firm against the werewolves or any other threat our population might face. "Adrienne and I'll go up the mountain and see if we can't head off any werewolf fighting," I continued. "If it was just a bunch of drunks spouting off Friday night, then we'll come back home, and no one will be the wiser."

"Before I say yes on this, I need to know your plan." Cassie scowled. "Tell me how the pair of you are going to hold off a dozen or more werewolves from attacking Clinton's compound."

Adrienne grinned. "Animals. It's what I do. There are plenty of animals up on the mountain who will help me. Or maybe I'll bring a couple of bears or break a lion or two out of the zoo. That would be fun."

I smothered a laugh. "And I'll hex them. Maybe they'll become hopelessly entangled in vines or get lost on their own mountain. Who knows what form a hex will take?"

Cassie shook her head and sighed. "Okay, but I want the pair of you to be safe. And the moment you're off that mountain, you need to call me and tell me you're both okay, or I'm hauling ass up there and setting some werewolf pants on fire."

I held up a hand and eyed Cassie solemnly. "We promise to be careful and call you right away. Promise."

And hopefully it would all be unnecessary. Hopefully the meeting tomorrow would go well, and we'd have peace and some compromise between the two alphas. Hopefully no one would make a move to attack Stanley. Hopefully Dallas would keep to whatever we agreed upon and keep the peace with Clinton.

If not…hopefully Eshu would agree to help me out, and I could ensure peace on the mountain with a powerful hex. And maybe a lion or two.

CHAPTER 15

SYLVIE

*M*onday morning, I forced myself out of bed early and made omelets with the remaining eggs and cheese while Eshu did his best to distract me and get me back to bed.

"I can't," I protested as he pulled my rear end against his erection. "It's Monday. I've got clients, then the werewolf meeting, then we need to go out with Adrienne to head off any potential attack on Clinton's compound."

"I'm looking forward to tonight." Eshu wiggled against my butt. "And I like your sisters. Well, except for the eldest one that wanted me to eat outside with the raccoon."

"Well, we're going up the mountain tonight with the one who talks to the raccoon," I told him. "Adrienne communicates with animals and can get them to do her bidding."

With Adrienne, it was less controlling animals and more that they liked her and happily did as she asked. I really didn't know if she actually *could* make an animal do something against its will or not.

"And what is my role in this adventure, beyond admiring my beautiful witch?" He kissed the side of my head.

This was so embarrassing. I hated to ask for help. He'd offered freely to assist me with the luck charms, but this was different. We'd only begun this…whatever the heck it was we had together, and I didn't want him thinking that I was using him in any way.

"I'm still weak, and I'm not sure I'll have enough strength to power a hex."

There. Hopefully he'd offer and I wouldn't have to actually ask.

He reached around me to flip the omelet, still keeping the other arm around my waist. "You will always have the strength you need. Whatever magic you decide to do, it will be sufficient."

"What if it's not?" I countered. "I'll be out there with Adrienne in a potentially dangerous situation. What if I can't cast a spell, or it's weak and ineffective?"

"Your spells will always be sufficient."

There was that word again. Sufficient. I really didn't like that word. Sufficient didn't give me any wiggle room, any buffer. And I didn't believe that anything I did on my own *would* be sufficient.

"But what if they're not? What if I can't do it and the werewolves attack Adrienne and me?"

He flipped the omelet again. "Then I'll save you. You first, and if your sister hasn't been killed and eaten by the werewolves, then I'll save her too."

"Werewolves don't eat people." He was going to make me say it. He was going to make me come right out and ask. Ugh, this was so embarrassing. "Can you…would you please let me have some of your energy like you did with the charms? Just in case?"

"There is no need for that. Have faith, Sylvie. Trust."

Trust in what? Myself? Him? Divine intervention?

"Sometimes the path is twisted," he continued, "and you

may fear you're going in the wrong direction, that you won't reach your destination. But remember that whatever direction you travel, it's always correct, and the destination you arrive at is the one you're destined for."

This was the wise, serious Eshu. I think I liked the laughing, frivolous one better—the one with the near-constant erection.

"So that's a 'no,' right?" I turned to face him, putting my hands on his chest and looking up into his dark eyes.

"Trust. Act intuitively. And have faith that your future will find you."

He leaned down and gave me a soft kiss, and as I pressed myself against him, I realized something. He was right. I needed to have faith that my luck would always be there for me, to catch me and make sure that even though I might fall, I wouldn't land on hard ground. Eshu might be there for me or he might not, but no matter how twisted the path, as he said, in the end I'd reach my destination. That destination might not be the one I set out for, but it would be the correct one for me.

Maybe my magic wouldn't fully return. Maybe it wouldn't be the same. But either way, I *was* lucky, I was alive, and I was in the arms of a demon—or whatever—who lit me up inside.

We ate breakfast, lingering over coffee as we chatted about my family, game night, what music we liked, then I managed to resist Eshu's attempts at a sexy shower, and got ready to head to the office.

"Call in sick," he urged, pulling me to him as I grabbed my purse and keys.

"I called in sick for two weeks while I was on Cassie's couch," I told him, pushing his roving hands from my breasts. "I need to be at work, especially today. Aren't you expected somewhere as well?"

Didn't the demon have work he was supposed to be doing? He'd been in and out of Cassie's place several times a day delivering and receiving messages, so I assumed he had messages to deliver to the wrong person.

"I've got some communications to take to heaven, then a few that need to go to the third circle. It can wait." He leaned in nibble my earlobe. "They can wait forever for all I care."

The guy had no work ethic, but honestly, this seemed to be the way all the denizens of hell acted. Lucien had pretty much ignored whatever duties he had until Hadur had given him shit for being a spoiled, entitled, lazy brat. And it's not like I'd seen Hadur do anything since he got out of that summoning circle. Two hundred years trapped in there and you would think the guy would have a huge backlog of wars or something to get going on, but no. Instead, he was forging knives to sell at one of the hunting stores in town. And I was pretty sure Lucien's recent bluster over his job was a load of bull and just busywork to make him look important. It seemed to me that hell pretty much just ran on its own without all this intervention, and I got the idea heaven was the same. So maybe those messages for Eshu really *could* wait for a few hours. Or days.

But my work couldn't. So, I kept pushing his hands away, gave him a quick kiss that almost convinced me to cancel my first appointment, then headed out to my office before I changed my mind.

I saw two clients, ate lunch, saw one more, then walked back to my house to get in my car and drive to the neutral zone Cassie had chosen for this meeting. It was outside the town wards at a McDonald's by the mall. There were quite a few humans in line, ordering late lunches or drinks. I got a soda and went through the door into the kids' area where clusters of tables and chairs surrounded a play structure with slides and padded platforms to climb on. A bored mom sat reading a book off to the side while two little girls shrieked and crawled through the tubes connecting the slides.

It was perfect. We were outside the safety of the town wards, so the werewolves would feel exposed. Add to that the fact that we were in a very public place, and in a room where children played, and the whole venue ensured the werewolves would be on their best behavior. Normally I'd think this was too much as I liked clients to have the freedom to express frustration and emotion, but with werewolves, frustration and emotion quickly led to flying fists and broken bottles as weapons. A children's play area in a fast food restaurant would keep that all under control.

I walked around the room, putting the button charms at each of the four corners. I could feel their energy, their power, reaching out to fill the room and beyond. It made me smile to think that these were a combination of both Eshu and me, a reminder of how very well we seemed to mesh together.

I liked him. I more than liked him. I liked him in my bed, in my life, in my house. I liked him at Sunday family dinner, and my game, and just lounging around. He made me happy.

Done with the charms, I headed back to the table I'd picked out for us and arranged the chairs, sitting down with my soda and my notebooks. I'd just gotten organized when Dallas and Clinton entered the room, bringing so much tension with them that the mother looked up from her book and sent them a wary glance.

I'll admit it was incredibly amusing to see the werewolves sitting on the too-small, brightly colored, plastic chairs. They each had a bag with burgers and fries and a drink in hand— all to look like they belonged here in the McDonald's, if not in the kids' play area. Werewolves loved eating just as much as they loved winning stuff in raffles, so both Dallas and

Clinton pulled the food out of the bags the moment they sat down.

"Damn it, I said no pickles," Clinton grumbled as he picked them off his burger and set them aside.

"You did. I heard you." Dallas inspected his own sandwich. "She got mine right at least. No pickles. No onions."

"Humans." Clinton sighed and reassembled his sandwich sans pickles. "This kinda thing is the reason I don't like to go outside the wards. I'm gonna end up with indigestion from those things."

"Better get used to things outside the wards, because you're soon gonna be living here... or be dead," Dallas replied.

"Excellent segue into the topic at hand," I jumped in before Clinton could reply and escalate the situation. "You guys eat while I sum things up and go over some rules, then we'll start the discussion."

I went over the usual—no interrupting, everyone has a chance to respond in turn. By the time I'd summed up the situation, the werewolves were done with their late lunch and sipping their sodas.

"Clinton, I want you to go first. I want you to say what *you* want in terms of your pack. Your ideal situation."

He took a long slurp of his soda and sat back. "I want a pack with different rules than what Dallas has. I want enough territory on Heartbreak Mountain for us to live and farm and hunt. I want my pack members to be able to come and go, to visit their friends and family in Dallas's compound."

I turned to the other werewolf. "And you, Dallas?"

"I want him dead and in the ground," he shot back.

I held up a hand for Clinton to remain silent and spoke to Dallas. "Really? Your son? The man you raised from a pup, who you watched grow? Your strong, assertive, take-no-shit son? You truly want him dead?"

Clinton wasn't a model son by human terms. Dallas had had to bail him out of the Accident jail any number of times for getting into fights in town, but as much as he'd complained, the werewolf alpha had been proud of his son's rabble-rousing ways. Werewolves liked troublemakers, as long as they were making trouble outside the pack. I knew that Dallas loved and admired his son, and that it would pain him terribly to see him dead. And I was counting on that to help him to bend a little, just a little, and compromise here today.

Dallas glared over at his son. "You shoulda challenged me. That's how it's done. That's how we always do it. Then I would be respecting you and not dealing with the embarrassment of my only pup being a cowardly traitor. *And* being accused of being weak and soft because I didn't go take you out that first week and nip this in the bud."

"I'da been dead if I'da challenged you," Clinton shot back. "You're stronger than me. Even on your deathbed you'll probably be stronger than me. My goal wasn't to end up bleeding out on the ground, it was to lead, to make a place where things were different for werewolves who wanted a different sort of pack, not to die by your hands for nothing."

"At least that way your death would have had meaning," Dallas growled. "It would have been honorable, according to our traditions. Now you'll die a coward and a traitor. That's not what I wanted for you. That's not what I wanted for my son."

"You might kill me, and you might kill my pack, but the damage has been done and there's no going back," Clinton snapped. "Twenty wolves risked their lives to go with me rather than continue to follow you, and there's plenty more in your pack that are on the fence. Kill me and my pack and maybe you'll get peace for another year or two, but things are going to change whether you want them to or not, old man."

The two little girls in the play equipment squealed with laughter over something. The door suddenly opened and in poured a dozen children, all wearing party hats and shouting as they tore off their shoes, threw them at the cubby, and raced for the slides. Three adults followed them in, carrying boxes of cupcakes and handfuls of presents.

What. The. Heck. Cassie had told me she'd ensured there wouldn't be any parties going on during our meeting. The manager had said they wouldn't be able to reserve the room because it had to be available to patrons, but that there were no scheduled parties, and that this day and time usually found the play area empty or with only one or two kids.

I eyed the luck charms in the corners, thinking that two weeks ago, this sort of thing wouldn't have happened.

The loud chaos of the excited kids did break the tension, though. The werewolves shifted in their ridiculously small seats, eyeing the partygoers nervously. It was a reminder that here, outside the wards, they were vulnerable and subject to human laws that wouldn't take their culture into consideration when deciding the fate of what humans saw as monsters.

"Dallas, I'm going to ask again—in an ideal world, what would you want? If you could turn back time, have things different, wave a magic wand over the whole situation, what would you want? Because I doubt it's your son dead."

The werewolf took a few deep breaths then glanced over at the children once more before meeting my gaze. "I'd want Clinton to come back to my pack and endure punishment for what he did. I want him to be a good and reasonably obedient wolf. To uphold our culture and traditions. When I get too old to be running things, he'd act in my stead, honoring me and respecting my leadership status. Then when I'm dead, he'll take over as alpha and keep with our customs."

These two were still miles apart, but at least I'd gotten Dallas to back off his war-chant.

"I can't do that, Da." Clinton's voice was husky and gruff, barely audible over the delighted screams of the children. "You changed things from the way Old Dog Butch did them. You kept the traditions and customs that you felt truly meant something to our people while changing the things you felt needed changing. Why can't you accept that I want change too? That I want a pack where things are done differently?"

"Then wait to do that after I'm dead and gone," Dallas snapped, nervously eyeing one of the parents who was hanging up a birthday banner.

"That's not fair when we've got wolves in our pack that want change now, not in fifty or sixty years. Just because they're not physically strong enough to kill you in a challenge fight, does that mean their wishes don't matter? That they shouldn't have a say in how things are run in the pack?" Clinton scooted his chair in farther, cringing when a nearby child let out a particularly high-pitched squeal.

The older werewolf bristled. "You mean voting and all that shit like they do in town with the mayor? Because that is *not* the way we werewolves do things."

"No, I don't mean voting. I just mean that if a lot of wolves want something different, then maybe they should be heard. Maybe we should be changing things. The alpha is a leader, Da. He's strong to protect the pack, but he's also there to serve them and make their lives better."

"I do that." Dallas' eyes glowed an eerie yellow, which thankfully neither the playing children nor their parents seemed to notice. "I take care of my people. I make sure the submissive and weak ones aren't driven out or killed. I let werewolves choose their own mates and take their time about it. There's no need to throw our traditions into the trash to do that, though."

I held up a hand to halt them both. "So, Dallas, you're not opposed to some change as long as you feel the important traditions and culture of the pack are upheld, right?" I waited for his nod. "Then let's hear what changes Clinton feels need to happen right now and discuss them."

Clinton nodded, shifting uneasily as a boy ran past him. "I think we need our pups to all attend the schools in Accident so they learn how to act around those who aren't werewolves and maybe make some friends outside the pack."

"That's a choice I'm not gonna take away from parents." Dallas glared at his son. "Some werewolves think their pups will pick up bad habits in those schools, that they'll end up disrespecting pack traditions and maybe even wind up like that Shelby, screwing a troll and leaving her pack behind."

"Plenty of werewolves went to those schools and didn't shack up with a troll. Parlay went to school in Accident from kindergarten through high school, and she's a loyal pack member, mated to Beaker and having his pup."

"That's gotta be a choice for the parents, though."

"Then make it an obvious choice. Financial incentives. Other pack incentives. Make it so parents *want* to send their pups to school in town because we need to start getting used to being with others that ain't werewolves. I mean, look at us, Da." Clinton waved a hand around. "We're sitting here at the edge of our seats, nervous as all heck around humans, terrified of a bunch of children. Two hundred years of near isolation hasn't done us any good."

"I ain't scared of the children," Dallas shot back. Then he proceeded to give those same children an anxious glance.

"It's not just schools, though. We need to re-think our traditions of fated mates."

"You're going too far now, boy," Dallas roared. Actually, it was a soft, almost whispered roar because he clearly didn't want to upset the kids and have them cry or draw the attention of the parents who were beginning to eye us suspiciously. "We're werewolves. Our inner wolves bond to our fated mates, and we join with them for life, outside of a few exceptions."

Clinton rolled his eyes. "And then the men screw around like crazy. How is that supportive of a 'fated mate' marriage? We're not a huge pack. What if someone doesn't find their fated mate? What if they just settle and choose a mate because they need one and want pups? Like you and my mother?"

Dallas bristled, and I once again held out a hand. "What are you proposing, Clinton? Do you want an easier path to divorce? Rules around fidelity for both partners? What?"

He fidgeted with his soda cup a bit before responding. "I still think the whole thing with Shelby and that troll is disgusting and abnormal. When she was found out, I'd agreed that she should have been locked in the compound and maybe even forced to mate with a proper werewolf. But...there's no fated mate for me in the pack, Da. I know every female werewolf in Accident. I've slept with darned near every female wolf in Accident. None of them is my mate. None. What if my fated mate is out here, beyond the wards? What if she's not even a werewolf?"

Dallas paled. "Werewolves outside the wards are wild and undisciplined. They've been driven by fear of humans to live alone or in small packs. They've lost their traditions and all sense of who they are. They're nothing more than animals pretending to be human. There's no fated mate for you out here. And there sure as hell isn't a fated mate for you among the trolls, or fae, or anyone else in Accident."

"I think you might have found your fated mate in Tink," Clinton told his father. "From what I've heard, your pairing with her is nothing like it was with my mother. Would you deny me the same? Would you deny those who have risked everything to join my pack the same? You found your love. Why can't we?"

"You're just too picky. If you opened your eyes a bit, I'm sure you could find your fated mate in the pack. Or just be unmated. You've got plenty of time before I die and you're alpha. Stay unmated. Screw whoever you like. Mate later."

"Does that mean you'd truly welcome Clinton and the others back into the pack?" I asked Dallas, envisioning a prodigal son type homecoming. "If you can both come to an agreement on these two things, then perhaps you can reconcile and all be part of one pack again."

Dallas let out a whoosh of a breath. "I could do that, although I'd need to disown Clinton to save face. Maybe in a few decades I can un-disown him if he's proven himself to be a dutiful and changed werewolf."

"No." Clinton's voice was firm. "I like leading my own pack. I'm not compromising on these key points and coming back to be a whipping boy, scoffed and jeered at for a few decades. These werewolves took a huge risk to come with me. I'm not going to betray their trust just to come crawling back to you. I'm staying with my pack, live or die."

Both werewolves stood, and Dallas jabbed a finger at his son. "Then our meeting here is over. Prepare your people because by the end of the week, they'll all be dead."

Right on the tail of that ominous speech, a little boy tripped over a piece of carpet, sending a cupcake flying into the alpha werewolf's face. It hit him right on the nose, splatting blue icing and sprinkles all over his skin and dropping down to smear food along the front of his shirt and pants.

Clinton laughed. Dallas stepped forward and drew back to punch the other werewolf, but before I could intervene, he stepped on one of the balls that had escaped the ball pit and fell hard onto the floor.

"Mister? Mister?" Clinton's laughter died abruptly as he turned to stare in horror at the little boy tugging at his sleeve with a sticky hand. "I gotta poop."

Clinton jerked his arm free, eyes wide as he spun away from the child. As he stepped back, he tripped over his father and also hit the floor, knocking an entire box of cupcakes over on top of himself. The kids screamed, a few began to cry, and the parents frantically tried to save any remaining cupcakes, glaring at the two werewolves who scrambled to their feet and raced for the door.

I ended up buying cookies and milkshakes for the party-goers in restitution for the smashed cupcakes. Then I collected my charms and headed out. I had thought we were making progress, but perhaps the werewolf situation was more than a luck witch trained in mediation could handle. Sometimes two people wouldn't budge. I had really hoped that Dallas and Clinton could find common ground, but it hadn't happened.

I drove over to Cassie's to give her the bad news. She'd taken to working from home a few days a week, juggling her lawyer job and her responsibilities to the town all at once. I found her with her files spread across the kitchen table, Lucien nowhere in sight. Grabbing a drink from the fridge, I sat down, carefully avoiding looking at the empty spot where the microwave had once stood.

"Looks like there's war on the mountain," I told her glumly. "Not just tonight, either. Dallas plans to wipe out Clinton and his pack by the end of the week."

Cassie shot me a sympathetic glance. "I'm sorry, Sylvie."

"I really don't know what more I can do." I sighed. "Dallas is so stuck on his pride. He claims it's about holding to their traditions, but I think it's more that Clinton disappointed and embarrassed him by taking off with a portion of the pack and not even giving him the courtesy of a challenge. He'd let Clinton and the others return, but they don't want to return. They want to remain autonomous with their own territory. Things got heated, then everything went sideways Three Stooges style, with falling and getting smashed with cupcakes, and kids needing to poop."

"What?" Cassie stared, open-mouthed.

"I know. I'm sorry. I tried my best, but you were right. I think the only thing that's gonna work with these guys is threats, and even then, we'll get sucked into fighting and probably some retaliation."

"No." Cassie waved away my statement. "Honestly, I didn't expect this to work, but you're good at what you do, and I figured it was worth a shot. I mean the kids pooping cupcakes and stuff. What the heck is that about?"

"Not pooping cupcakes. The cupcakes and the poop were separate things—at least, I hope they were separate things. A dozen kids showed up right as we got started and were racing around playing and yelling. It was some sort of birthday party."

Cassie frowned. "No. I talked to the manager and he specifically told me he'd block off the time so there wouldn't be any parties."

"Well, he must have gotten the days mixed up or something, because there was definitely a party. Some kid fell and smacked Dallas in the face with a cupcake, then he stepped on a ball from the ball pit and went down. Then the kid that needed to poop decided that Clinton of all people should take him to the restroom. Clinton backed away and fell over Dallas who was on the floor and upended a whole box of cupcakes. I've never seen two werewolves move so fast. They were covered in cupcake icing. And you know how nervous they are around humans—especially human children. I had to stay and make nice with the parents, buying milkshakes and cookies to make up for the cupcakes."

Cassie shook her head and laughed. "Sounds like a mess. A perfect storm of bad luck." I sucked in a breath at her comment and she reached out for my arm. "Crap. I'm sorry, Sylvie. I didn't mean to imply anything. It was just a comedy of errors, not anything to do with luck."

Maybe it had a lot to do with luck. I pulled the button charms out of my purse and looked at them. The old me, pre-death, wouldn't have had any of this happen. The old luck witch me wouldn't have had her mediation interrupted by a mistakenly scheduled birthday party or had the cupcake-smashing, tripping-and-falling chaos at the end, either.

I'd made these charms, and Eshu charged them. What an idiot I'd been. My sisters might be able to use demon energy to supplement their powers, but Eshu wasn't really a demon. I should have known. He was such a contrarian. My charms had probably been charged and reversed to be bad luck charms instead of good luck ones.

"Tell me what you think of these," I said, handing the button charms to Cassie.

Her mouth formed a surprised "o." "Holy crap, these are charged to the max. But it's not your energy." She squinted at them, rolling the buttons between her fingers. "Is it? It doesn't look like your energy."

I blinked back tears, hating to admit the very thing I'd been trying to hide from my sisters for the last two weeks. "It's not my energy. I can't work my magic anymore, Cassie. Not since I died. I can do the technical part of it, but when I go to bring a spell to life, nothing happens. It's like I'm not even a witch anymore. I'm afraid I'll never be able to work my magic again, that it will never come back."

She dropped the charms onto the table and came around to gather me into a huge hug. "Oh, hon. It'll all be okay. Just give yourself some time to heal. You're pushing too hard. You're trying to do things when you're still recovering from what happened. You just need more time, sweetie."

I laughed, feeling a few tears slip free. "I'm not coming back to stay on your couch, just in case that's what you're about to propose. Much as I appreciate you taking care of me, I really need to be back in my own house, trying to get my life together again."

She pulled back to smile at me, running a hand over my hair like she'd done when we were kids. "Okay. Just be patient with yourself. And stop worrying. You're a witch. You'll always be a witch. It'll all come back with time."

What if it didn't? What if I spent the rest of my life fatigued halfway through the day? Not able to cast spells? Having to rely on Glenda's smoothies just to get through the week?

But I'd worried Cassie enough with my fears. It would only upset her that she couldn't do something to fix me with a snap of her fingers. I'd heal or I wouldn't. No sense in continuing to cry over it.

I wiped my eyes and pointed over to the button charms. "Eshu helped me power those up. I figured if Lucien helped with your magic and Hadur helped with Bronwyn's, that he could help with mine."

Cassie grimaced. "But Eshu is...different."

"You're telling me." I laughed. "Everything around him turns into a slapstick comedy. I should have realized any charm he powered would probably do the same. Instead of drawing luck to the meeting today, I drew bad luck."

Cassie pursed her lips. "I wouldn't say *bad* luck. I mean, the birthday party totally threw the werewolves off their game. And the falling down and cupcakes and kid needing to poop defused a tense situation before it could turn into a fight, *and* before Dallas and Clinton said things they couldn't take back. Maybe they *are* luck charms, only not in the way you usually define luck."

It hit me that Cassie was right. But even if they were Eshu-type luck charms, I was definitely going to think twice before I asked him to power my magic in the future.

CHAPTER 16

SYLVIE

"*W*here are the lions?" Eshu asked, peering around Adrienne as if he suspected she was hiding them behind her back. My sister had arrived right at ten-thirty, giving us plenty of time to head up the mountain and be in place before any midnight werewolf attack took place.

"I couldn't bring them. My truck is acting up and they won't fit in my Fiat. Besides, it was steak night at the zoo and neither of them wanted to miss that. I'll just have to make do with whatever animals are available up on the mountain tonight."

I grimaced, thinking this was an omen, a warning that tonight was not going to go as planned and would probably end up being a shitshow of epic proportions. But what could I do? Even if Ophelia were here to give me a glimpse into the future, I couldn't exactly call the whole thing off and just allow Dallas's group to attack Clinton.

They'd been warned, and I had no doubt that the smaller pack was alert and ready, but Dallas had numbers on his side, and I knew how this night would go if we did nothing but stay at home.

"We'll take my car," I told the two, knowing the three of us would have an uncomfortable ride squished into Adrienne's tiny Fiat. I grabbed my purse and, at the last moment, stuffed the button charms into my pocket, just in case. They'd delivered a chaotic sort of luck at the McDonald's, but hopefully they could serve in an emergency tonight as well.

For the first time in weeks, I could feel a tiny trickle of magic like the brush of a feather along my skin. It both thrilled and frightened me. My power was returning, but this tiny bit wouldn't do much against a mob of werewolves. I'd need more. But I tried to trust in whatever that my powers would be sufficient, that things would turn out right. Hopefully Eshu was right and this twisty path I was on wouldn't lead to a dead end—emphasis on *dead*.

We headed out of town and as far up the mountain as I felt we could go without detection, then we hopped out and headed into the forest on foot.

A mile in, I was thinking this wasn't such a great idea after all. I'd downed the rest of Glenda's smoothie, and I *did* feel much stronger than I had this time last week, but not quite up to a late-night hike up a mountain. We veered off the dirt road and onto a set of winding trails as we kept ourselves on the downward side of the wind to avoid detection from the werewolves' sensitive noses.

When we were a reasonable distance from Clinton's compound, we halted, trying to keep the element of surprise on our side. It wasn't just someone sniffing us out that I worried about. Clinton had wolves in the woods keeping their eyes peeled and ears perked for intruders. Hopefully my luck would hold, and no one would know we were here.

"What are you planning on using, Adrienne?" I asked, leaning against a tree for a bit of rest.

"I've got sentries to give us notice of when they're coming and to let me know from what direction," Adrienne said. "Starlings. They really get a bad rap, you know, but they're always willing to help. And they work well together. Two hundred of them are going to be giving us a hand—or wing— tonight. Once the werewolves get here, I'm going to use insects and birds to hopefully get them to turn around and go back home. How about you?"

I fingered the buttons in my pocket. "A hex. I'm targeting plant life."

And I wasn't sure what form that hex would take or how helpful it would be. I was hoping for some fur-pene- trating thorny bushes, hedges full of briars—that sort of thing. And if I couldn't manage it myself, I'd take a chance and use the power from the button charms to try some- thing else.

"How about you?" Adrienne turned to Eshu.

"I'm just here to admire my couch-witch's amazing back- side. When this is all over, I'm hoping we can have sex on a nice patch of moss somewhere under the stars."

"I might need him," I told Adrienne, unsure exactly how I expected Eshu to help. He wasn't going to help me power my spells, and his sole contribution seemed to be telling me I was absolutely capable of doing this. Maybe I'd brought him along for a confidence boost? Moral support? To pull my amazing backside out of the fire if needed?

"Have you got any kind of demon weaponry?" Adrienne asked him. "Pitchfork? That sort of thing?"

"I got my pitchfork right here." Eshu grabbed his crotch. "I guess I can use it as a weapon. I've never tried that before."

"I'm thinking you need to keep your pitchfork in your pants," I told him. "At least until we're back home." I'd gotten rather fond of it and didn't want to see it sliced up by were-wolf claws.

"It used to be bigger," Eshu commented in a casual tone as if he were discussing the weather and not his penis. "A long time ago I used it as a bridge to help some people cross a river."

Adrienne snort-laughed and I rolled my eyes. "Your dick is big, but it's not bridge-over-a-river big," I told him.

"It used to be," he insisted. "But those stupid travelers wouldn't cross one at a time. They were in such a hurry that they all piled on my giant dick-bridge, and it broke so they all fell into the river and drowned."

"That sounds painful," Adrienne said.

Eshu nodded. "It was. Thankfully my trouser snake is still an impressive length. The lesson here is never to let anyone use your genitals to cross a river."

"I'll remember that." I shook my head and chuckled.

"You're weird," Adrienne told Eshu. "You'll fit right in with our family. And you'll certainly make Sunday night family dinner a whole lot more interesting."

I smiled to hear my sister say that. It was good to know I had one family member on my side as far as Eshu went. Ophelia would always back me up, but I knew she was perplexed as to why I was with the demon. And Cassie...well, maybe someday she'd accept Eshu, although I doubted she'd ever be a fan.

Adrienne tilted her head and put a finger to her lips. "They're coming," she whispered. "Up the main road to the south of us. We're downwind, and I'll ask some deer to cover our noise as we move closer."

I nodded, and we made our way closer to the road, trying to be as quiet as we could. We weren't in place more than ten minutes when I saw the mob marching up the road.

No advanced scouts. No attempt at stealth. Either Dallas

was incredibly sure that he'd be able to easily take the other werewolves down without any effort at surprise on their part, or he was secretly hoping to provide enough warning to his son's pack that they could be prepared and maybe retreat off the mountain.

I was hoping for the latter.

Closing my eyes, I mouthed the words of my spell and felt the small thread of energy spark to life then die out. Sliding my hand in my pocket, I touched the button charms and tried again. This time, the energy roared through me with such force that it would have knocked me on my back if Eshu hadn't been behind me.

He put a steadying hand on my shoulder, and I drew in a ragged breath, hoping the spell worked as I'd intended.

Adrienne gave me a nod and wiggled her fingers. Instantly, the air swarmed with hundreds of hornets, every one of them descending on the werewolves. I clapped a hand over my mouth to stifle a laugh as the werewolves danced around, cursing and slapping themselves as they tried to ward off the stinging insects. Some of them dove into the nearby bushes that I'd hexed, only to shriek as they found themselves in huge patches of wolfsbane. A few of the werewolves raced forward instead of retreating, and with a wiggle of Adrienne's fingers, a murmuration of starlings swooped from the sky, dropping a thick load of bird poop on the werewolves. It was working. The mob of werewolves turned and ran back home with only one werewolf remaining to shout after his fleeing pack.

It was at that exact moment when my luck ran out. The wind shifted, and just as Dallas was starting to head after the others, he stiffened, turning around and lifting his nose to the air.

I froze, but the gig was up. Dallas snarled, his eyes

glowing bright yellow as he turned and looked straight toward where we were hiding.

I'd knew there had been a chance that the werewolves would scent us out and know we were behind this. Even if they didn't, I still knew there was a good chance they'd put two and two together and realize that a swarm of stinging insects and dive-bombing birds were magically coordinated. I just assumed Dallas would realize that we Perkins witches weren't going to let this sort of violence happen inside our wards any longer, and that he'd concede the battle to us, if not the war. What I didn't anticipate was how incredibly pissed off he'd be.

I'd seen werewolves angry before, but never this angry. A sane, rational Dallas would realize that if he killed us, he'd be sealing his fate, but this wasn't a sane, rational Dallas. This was a werewolf who'd steeled himself to possibly kill his son and former packmates tonight, only to be stung by dozens of hornets, covered in boils from the wolfsbane, and coated with a large quantity of slimy bird crap. I reached inside my pocket to grip the button charms, hoping there was enough juice in them to get the three of us out of this.

Dallas took a step toward us, claws lengthening from his fingers, his jaw extending outward with the appearance of huge sharp teeth. "This. Is. War," he roared.

Crap. I squeezed the button charms, trying to do something, anything. Make him slip and fall and injure himself enough to give us time to flee. Anything.

"Wish I'd brought a lion," Adrienne muttered.

"Lion. Got it," Eshu said.

The words were followed up by a roar that answered Dallas's, and I felt myself knocked aside as a giant tawny-furred animal leapt past me and into the road.

It was a lion, but not like any lion I'd ever seen at the zoos. He was six feet at the shoulder and probably around a thousand pounds. He was a lion the size of a huge horse, and he was chasing Dallas down the road away from us and back home.

Eshu. The guy could shapeshift. Now that would have been a good thing to know before we headed out on this excursion. But I wasn't too upset because he'd clearly saved us—for now.

"Think he'll kill the werewolf?" Adrienne asked as the two figures vanished into the dark.

"I hope not." I winced. "Either way we're screwed. Dallas caught our scent, and I doubt he's going to let this go."

Adrienne stood up and brushed the dirt off her jeans. "Well, he's got a choice. He can tell everyone in the pack we thwarted his attack plans, or he can keep mum about it and take revenge on us some other time. Or he can let the whole thing go and be grateful we gave him an excuse not to have to kill his son."

"For tonight," I reminded her, getting up as well. "He could easily regroup and do this again. We can't be up here every night protecting Clinton's compound. Next time he'll be ready for us, and we might not have Eshu-the-giant-lion to drive him off."

"Speaking of which, that was freaking awesome."

I agreed, and as we headed back to the car, I thought about how amazing Eshu had been. He'd let us take the lead but jumped in when we were in trouble and needed help. And I'd done magic. Yes, I'd needed to steal some energy from the button charms, but I'd still managed to pull off a successful spell. That meant a lot and made me feel as if someday I might actually be back to normal—or at least as normal as a witch who'd died could ever be.

The pair of us were on high alert as we walked, but I still nearly jumped out of my skin to see a figure standing next to our car. It was only when he turned to me and smiled that I realized it was Eshu.

Running, I jumped into his arms and planted a kiss on him. I was aiming for his lips but in my enthusiasm missed and instead ended up kissing his nose instead.

"Thank you. He was so angry, and I wasn't sure what he was going to do to us, and I was all tapped out of energy. If you hadn't jumped in, I don't know what would have happened to us."

"Hey! I wasn't tapped out. I was planning on...I don't know, summoning some earthworms or something." Adrienne came up behind me and crushed me in the middle of a quick three-way hug. "Thank you, Eshu. You were even better than the lions at the zoo. But don't tell them that. They're real divas."

"I wasn't going to let my couch-witch get mauled by a werewolf." Eshu placed a kiss on my forehead. "Or her sister, either. Now if that Cassie sister had been here, I might have decided on a different sort of action, especially if she had Lucien with her."

I laughed. "If Cassie had been here with Lucien, they would have been fully able to take care of Dallas themselves. She's more powerful than the rest of us, even without Lucien by her side."

Eshu smoothed my hair. "You're more powerful than you think. Your luck isn't just magic, it's part of who you are, and no exploding microwave can take that away from you."

I looked into his dark eyes and felt something beyond lust. Yes, he was funny. He made me laugh, made me dissolve into a puddle with one touch, but the gossamer strands that pulled us together had strengthened over the last few days and I realized I really wanted him by my side. Maybe forever.

Adrienne cleared her throat, yawning as I turned to look at her. "I'm beat and I need to deal with a vulture problem tomorrow. Can we get going? You guys can continue this love-fest once we're back in town and I'm on my way home."

I gave Eshu another quick kiss, this one on his lips, then dug my keys out of my pocket. Yes, I totally wanted to continue this love-fest, but I'd need to do more than drop Adrienne off at her car out front of my house. I'd need to call Cassie and let her know we were safe—*and* let her know what a complete and utter mess we'd made of things.

CHAPTER 17

SYLVIE

"So, I really screwed things up," I told Cassie.

We were meeting at the diner early in the morning. Cassie had her business suit on and was shoveling down a plate of scrambled eggs like she hadn't eaten in a week. I was in my usual jeans and tank top, fiddling with a plate of pancakes that I just couldn't muster the appetite to eat.

Eshu had done his best to quell my anxiety last night, but I was still fretting over it all. Our actions had delayed the attack on Clinton's pack, but not stopped it. And I was sure we'd made an enemy of Dallas who, although he'd never been a huge fan before, had at least been somewhat cooperative with us.

"Sylvie, relax," Cassie said around a mouthful of eggs. "Things have been heading in this direction with the were-wolves ever since I granted Shelby asylum and protection as a lone wolf. Actually, things have been heading in this direction for over a hundred years. I'm just the first witch with the attitude to tell those furry jerks to bring it."

"I'm worried this is going to pit Dallas's pack against all of us. He'll see it as us taking sides, as an attack. He said it was war."

Cassie rolled her eyes. "The drama. Like hornet stings, wolfsbane, and bird poop are a big deal to werewolves. You said Eshu did nothing more than chase Dallas back home, so they're fine this morning except for their pride and a few boils from the wolfsbane. If that's enough to start a war, then I would have burned them to a crisp over the thousand bar fights they've started over the last few years."

I chewed on my lip and scooted bits of pancake around my plate.

Cassie let out a whoosh of a breath. "Look, I'll call him this morning once he's had time to cool down. I'll let him know that we're not going to allow any war inside the wards, whether that's in town or on the mountain."

"I hate that we need to deliver an ultimatum," I told her. "I wanted us to find a compromise, a way for Dallas and Clinton to come to an agreement and have both packs live in harmony with the rest of Accident."

"I love that you're so optimistic, that you're always striving for a collaborative solution to every problem. When we were kids, you were always the peacemaker. We need that in this town, we need you. I need you. But there are times when a heavy hand is needed, and I truly think this is one of those times. I'll get in Dallas's face over this, and if he doesn't back down, he'll find that hornets and bird poop are the least of his worries."

I understood what Cassie was saying, but I also saw the long-term repercussions of that sort of approach. There would always be an us-versus-them atmosphere between the werewolves and the rest of Accident, and it might take us centuries more to ease back from that. I'd worked so hard to understand them, to gain their trust as clients. I didn't want to have to threaten them to achieve peace; I wanted them to come willingly to it, understanding that it was in their own best interests as well as ours.

But maybe I was a fool to want that when Dallas was so set on a violent solution.

"Stop beating yourself up over last night." Cassie reached out and gripped my hand with hers, stilling my fork on the plate. "You saved lives, and honestly, sweetie, you didn't make things worse. It's all going to be okay."

It wasn't. No matter what Cassie or Eshu said, I had a horrible feeling in my gut that it wasn't going to be okay. At best, the werewolves would chafe under the threat of our combined might, taking pot shots at each other and continuing to do what they'd always done even farther from our gaze. I wanted a solution. I *needed* a solution. But Cassie was resigned to her course, and Eshu kept telling me to trust whatever, and that everything would work out in the end.

He wanted me to have faith, but after my death, I didn't have faith—not in me, not in anything.

I glanced down at my watch and pushed my plate away, sliding my hand from under Cassie's. "I've got to get going. I've got a client to meet this morning."

At least I *thought* I had a client to meet this morning. Tink might not show up if Dallas had told her what happened last night. Either way, I needed to be at my office, just in case.

"You didn't eat your breakfast," Cassie said, waving away my attempt to put some money on the table for the bill.

"I had a big dinner," I lied. Then I gave her a hug and a kiss on the cheek and headed out for my office, hoping that Tink would show up and that maybe after our session, I could convince her to let me know Dallas's mood and whether or not there was any hope in salvaging this huge mess I'd helped create.

CHAPTER 18

"*Y*ou've got to tell me what happened Monday at the mediation." Tink giggled and folded her legs up crosswise on her chair as she sipped her drink. "Dallas came home totally unnerved, covered in icing."

She'd showed up at my office right on time for her appointment with no mention whatsoever about what had happened last night. I guess Dallas had decided to keep that as well as my part in it a secret, and that he'd showered before coming to bed or Tink would be wondering why he was covered with hornet stings and bird poop.

"We met at a McDonald's playroom," I told her. "There wasn't supposed to be anyone there, but things got screwed up and in came this birthday party with a dozen kids. Let's just say chaos ensued and there was a bit of a disaster with the cupcakes."

Tink threw her head back and laughed. "Oh, Lord. Dallas don't like human kids at all. He don't like human adults either, but he's especially afraid of their kids."

I shook my head. "Not all werewolves are so nervous around humans, are they? I heard that you go outside the wards sometimes and don't seem traumatized when you get back."

"Oh, the first time I was scared to death, but it got easier each time afterward. You just have to get used to the humans and how they do things. It's different here in Accident, and it's really different in the compound up on the mountain. Most of us don't come into town all that often, and a good many of us have never been outside the wards in our lives. We're raised with stories of humans killing us or locking us up until we go moon-crazy. They're our boogieman stories, and unless a werewolf gets out and actually sees the human world, that's what they believe."

I shook my head. "So, what's your impression of life outside the wards?"

She shrugged. "I like humans. They're crazy and unpredictable and dangerous, but I like them. They've got good ideas, and some really good shopping and art, and I like how they live their lives. I kinda wish we could make the pack more like human life, but too many werewolves are stuck wanting things the old ways. Too many are afraid to change."

"Like Dallas?" I suggested.

She shot me a naughty grin. "Oh, Dallas is more open to change than he lets on. He mated me knowing what a total train wreck I am. He compromises on lots of things and is pretty intrigued by modern life. But he's alpha to a pack of traditionalists, and he feels like he needs to represent them. Plus, he doesn't like being wrong one bit, so you have to word things so they sound like they're his idea and that they'll benefit the pack. And he *is* afraid of humans. I don't think he's been outside the wards more than a dozen times in his life. I aim to change that."

I had no doubt in my mind that Tink would in fact change that. I thought about what she said and wondered if there was a way to spin this thing between Dallas and

Clinton where they both could compromise a bit, and no one would end up in a humiliating position.

Tink and I had a nice long session about the very unusual kink she'd read about somewhere, which frankly I did not quite understand. We finished up our session with a brainstorming session of less extreme, fun sexy-times things she could surprise Dallas with, then we both settled in for a cup of tea and a nice long gossip.

"I half expected you wouldn't come today," I confessed.

She grinned. "Because of what happened in the woods? Dallas didn't tell me about it, but I saw the bunch of them going out and I figured they were going to do a raid on Clinton's compound. When they all came running back, full of wolfsbane boils and covered with bird poop…well, it doesn't take a genius to realize witches were involved."

"You don't blame us? Because Dallas sure does."

She shrugged. "You didn't kill anyone or hurt them bad, and Dallas needs to know that he's not the big wolf he thinks he is. Yeah, I'm sure he's mad, but that's mostly 'cause he's embarrassed."

"I really screwed stuff up last night, didn't I?"

Tink looked at me over the rim of her mug. "I don't know. You did get them to turn back from attacking Clinton."

"And now they're focused on us witches. What's going to happen, Tink? You know the werewolves and Dallas better than I do. Are they going to cut themselves off even more from the rest of Accident? Declare the mountain a sovereign nation behind the wards? Attack us?"

She sat down her tea and eyed me for a long moment. "Are we still bound by all that privacy stuff?"

I scooted forward in my chair. The session was over, but I'd be happy to extend it and the confidentiality it ensured if it meant Tink would tell me something I could leverage to fix this mess.

"Yes. What you tell me stays between us."

She took a breath, blushing a bit. It made me wonder if we were going to discuss something weirder than lemon zesters and hemorrhoid cream.

"Dallas don't know what to do. He's stuck, Sylvie. He needs a way out, and if someone don't give it to him, he's gonna have to make a stand against you witches as well as keep on with this war against Clinton."

"I tried, Tink. I tried at the mediation session to find a solution between the two of them, and it didn't work. When I asked him where he'd be willing to compromise, he wouldn't budge. The closest he came to it was saying Clinton could come back and be disowned and punished, and of course Clinton wouldn't go for that."

"You need to give him the way out, Sylvie." She picked up her mug again and fiddled with it. "Dallas can't propose the solution because he looks weak if he compromises. The only way he can back down on this is if he's doing it to protect his pack against a bigger threat or as a boon because someone did something that went above and beyond to help the pack."

I thought of Eshu last night on the mountain. "Like if Clinton and his pack joined Dallas to fight off a pack of lions or save them from an erupting volcano or something," I mused.

"Exactly." She shifted in her chair, blushing again. "With Dallas, it's always a bit of carrot *and* stick. The carrot alone don't work, and the stick alone don't work. You need both."

He was already mad at me and Adrienne. It was logical to think the solution was for us witches to attack so Clinton and his father could bond over fighting us off, but I didn't want to go there. I didn't want to further fracture the relationship between the werewolves and us, and I didn't want the packs to withdraw even further from Accident as a whole. No, we needed an exterior threat for them to come together over.

And it would help if it wasn't just Clinton and his pack that helped, but us as well.

"Dallas doesn't want to kill Clinton. He doesn't want to go to war against you witches. He knows there's people in the pack that want things different, but he doesn't know how to give it to them without appearing weak. He's stuck, Sylvie."

"He's the alpha. Can't he just say he's changing things and that they need to deal? Isn't that pretty much what he did when he took over from Old Dog Butch?"

She flushed again. "It was easier to change things when he was the brand-new alpha. If he changes them now without a solid reason, he looks like he's weak. Dallas can't look weak. He needs to appear strong, confident, inflexible, wily, generous to those who are loyal, and protective of the pack."

I thought for a second, musing over what I could possibly do to give Dallas the out he needed.

Tink set down her mug and leaned forward. "It's exhausting for him. Always needing to be on, always needing to be the strong one. When someone gives him an opportunity to relax, to not be in charge for a few moments in private or behind the scenes, he's thrilled. He just can't have that sort of thing public, if you know what I mean."

Suddenly I did know what she meant. "So, you and Dallas...you both...?"

She nodded and shot me a sheepish grin. "I'm in charge in the bedroom. I plan everything. I tell him what to do, and he does it. It's glorious. And he loves it, but no one can know."

Male sexual submission was a common kink, but I'd honor confidentiality on this just as I always did with my clients because I could see how this wouldn't be acceptable in werewolf culture, especially with their alpha.

"If you can think of a way where Dallas owes you one, or owes Clinton one, or needs to unite with both Clinton and the witches to fend off a bigger foe, he'll jump at it." She picked up her mug of tea and finished it off. "Give him an out, Sylvie. He doesn't want to kill his son or other werewolves. He doesn't want a war with the witches. Give him an out."

CHAPTER 19

SYLVIE

"I don't know." Cassie eyed me. "It sounds pretty convoluted. If they find out it was us that staged this whole thing, we're even more screwed then we already are. And I don't like the idea of using Eshu."

I glanced over at the demon, who was rooting through Cassie's kitchen cabinets in search of a snack. He didn't seem to care that my sister was referring to him as if he wasn't even in the room with us.

"The werewolves know Lucien, Hadur, and Nash," I argued. "They don't know Eshu, and he can stage the attack so it doesn't blow back on us."

Her eyebrows went up. "This is Eshu we're talking about here. Something's going to go wrong. With Eshu, something always goes wrong."

"But then it always goes right," I insisted. "Well, maybe not in the third circle of hell, but other than that, things always seem to turn out right. Plus, I get the impression it doesn't really matter if Dallas thinks it was us or not. He needs an out. He's stuck and he needs us to provide a solution where he saves face and doesn't have to go to war with anyone or kill his son."

She nodded slowly. "Kind of like what happened with Tink."

"Exactly."

She let out a breath and sent the demon an annoyed glance. "Stop going through my kitchen cabinets and come over here. I need to know what sort of creatures or beings you can shapeshift into."

I winced at her tone. Cassie was always a bit bossy, but I really didn't like how she was speaking to my boyfriend.

Yeah, he was my boyfriend. And the thought made me all warm and tingly.

"I can take the form of anything," Eshu replied, starting to pull handfuls of spices out of a cabinet and putting them on the counter.

"It has to be something scary enough for the werewolves to need to work together and for them to want to accept our help," I mused.

"But it can't be a dragon, or a manticore, or a chimera, or anything we've got living in Accident," Cassie added. "I don't want any of the residents implicated in this."

Yeah, it wouldn't be good if Dallas came storming into town and accused Fernando of getting his dragon kin to attack them.

"Why can't I just be a demon?" Eshu had moved on to the cabinet with the boxed goods and proceeded to empty that one as well.

"Because then the werewolves will think Lucien is behind it," Cassie snapped.

I saw the mischievous glint in Eshu's eye, quickly hidden as he shoved his hand into a box of Cocoa Puffs and crammed the cereal into his mouth. I knew what that glint meant, and although it would be funny if he impersonated

Lucien and got the other demon into trouble, it wouldn't help our cause one bit.

"Let's think of something more interesting for you to shapeshift into," I told him. "How about a phoenix? Or a djinn—"

"Too much like a demon," Cassie interrupted.

"Or a fire elemental—"

"They'll think it's an ifrit."

I threw up my hands in exasperation. "An alien? A dinosaur?"

Cassie snapped her fingers. "A dinosaur. A big T-rex. That will work."

I wrinkled my nose, wondering if it really would work or not. I mean, there *were* no dinosaurs. Wouldn't the werewolves assume magic was involved if a T-rex stormed into the compound, and that we were involved?

"Like a skeleton T-rex? A museum fossil come to life?" I asked, thinking they'd surely blame Babylon for that one.

"No, like in *Jurassic Park*. They've barely been out to the human world in centuries. They'll buy it."

"You sure a phoenix wouldn't be better?" I pleaded.

Cassie waved her hand. "Nope. I don't want to set the forest on fire or anything. T-rex it is. Can you shapeshift into a T-rex?" she asked Eshu.

"Not now," I hastily told the demon. "She means is it possible for you to do that."

That gleam was back in his eyes, and I didn't trust that the guy wouldn't smash through the roof of the house by turning into a twenty-foot tall dinosaur just to annoy Cassie.

"Sure," he said through a mouthful of cereal.

"So, here's the plan." Cassie stood and began to pace. "You shapeshift into a T-rex. Then you go to Clinton's compound and stomp on a few sheds or houses something. Make sure no one's in them and that you don't hurt or kill any of the werewolves."

"You want me to check the houses before I stomp on them?" Eshu asked. "Like bend down and shove my head through the door just to make sure?"

I stifled a laugh and Cassie glared at him.

"Trust me, if you roar really loud before you do it, no one is going to be in their houses."

"Yeah, they'll all be shooting me or trying to claw me in half," Eshu shot back.

"You'll be forty feet long," Cassie informed him. "And you're a demon. Just...just roar really loud, kick a few trucks over and stomp a few houses, then run—but don't run too fast because they need to be able to follow you—run through the forest to Dallas's compound and do the same thing."

Eshu ate another handful of cereal. "How many bullets am I going to take during this little adventure? Stab wounds? Bite marks? Splinters from the houses and trees I'm stomping? Because it doesn't sound like you're going to let me defend myself here."

"I'm not. You're a demon. You'll be okay."

"Will you?" I asked him, concerned. He was right. The werewolves would shoot him, rake him with their claws, and bite him. And he might very well get splinters.

He sighed dramatically. "I've died before. There better be a really good offering, though."

That took Cassie aback. "You're dating my sister. You're living in the town. Why wouldn't you just help us?"

I knew Eshu would do it if I asked him, but I wanted Cassie to stop being such a jerk to him, so I sat back and kept my lips zipped.

"Because I don't like you and I don't do things for people I don't like. Unless they present me with an offering." He leaned against the counter and dug around in the cereal box.

Cassie turned to me, her expression pleading. I shrugged, giving her no help whatsoever.

"Wine?"

Eshu waved a hand for her to go on.

"A bottle of wine and a bottle of rum, and a box of cigars."

Eshu pursed his lips. "Eh."

"And you get to be at Sunday night dinner with the family," Cassie added.

"I already get to be there because Sylvie said so," Eshu countered.

"Then…" Cassie looked around the kitchen. "Wine, rum, cigars, and a quarter of beef from Woody's Butchery. And a pizza."

"With sardines?" Eshu asked.

Cassie shuddered. "With sardines."

"Deal." Eshu extended a Cocoa Puff dust-covered hand and Cassie reluctantly shook it.

"So, I'm supposed to turn into a raptor—"

"A T-rex," Cassie corrected.

"A T-rex. Then I roar, destroy Clinton's compound and kill a few of his packmates, then head to Dallas's—"

"No!" Cassie howled. "No killing."

"Destroy the compound, then head to Dallas's—"

"No, just a few houses and maybe a truck or two. Think kinder and gentler T-rex."

"I turn into Barney and sing about friendship and love, then I smash some houses and a few trucks—"

I laughed at Cassie's glare. "You've got to admit, psycho Barney would completely freak the werewolves out. Probably even more than a T-rex."

"No, a regular T-rex like in the *Jurassic Park* movie, only don't eat or kill anyone, and don't do too much property damage," Cassie told Eshu.

"How do I know when to stop?" he asked, eating another handful of cereal.

"I'll banish you," I told him, then laughed at his panicked expression. "Not really banish, silly. I'll cast a pretend spell telling you to go back to dinosaur island and never come back again."

"You're certain I'm not going to actually be sent to dinosaur island?" he asked with a worried frown.

There was no dinosaur island, and I was pretty sure Eshu couldn't be banished. It had to do with his whole "no rules apply to me, no one limits where I can go" spiel. Still, his concern—and his belief that I actually could perform that sort of spell—was cute.

"I promise." I held up a hand. "And if I accidently send you to dinosaur island, I swear that I'll come live with you there."

"Dressed as Wilma from *The Flintstones*?" He wiggled his eyebrows.

"With a fur outfit and a bone in my hair," I promised.

"You won't need to bring a bone, cause I've got all the bone you'll ever need."

Cassie rolled her eyes. "Okay, enough of that. We're set, right? Midnight you start with Clinton's compound, and we'll meet you at Dallas's compound to save the day."

"And I get my offerings when?" he asked.

"As soon as we're done." Cassie narrowed her eyes. "I'm not about to give them to you beforehand. Let's just say they're a guarantee that you're not going to screw this up."

"Don't worry, eldest sister witch, I will be the best, scariest T-rex ever. Just you remember to have my offerings ready because that's the deal and I'm not lenient when it comes to mortals who welsh on their deals, even if you are my beloved couch-witch's sister."

"I'll have it ready." Cassie stood and shooed us out of the kitchen. "Now get going. I've got some spells I need to work on for tonight if we're going to pull this off. Sylvie, I'll see you around ten?"

I nodded and headed out the door with Eshu. It wasn't until we got in the car that I realized he still had the box of Cocoa Puffs in his hands.

"Dude. I didn't think that was part of the deal." I pointed to the box.

He ate a handful. "Beloved couch-witch, cereal is *always* part of the deal."

CHAPTER 20

ESHU

I followed Sylvie to her eldest sister's house, then hung around while they discussed which spells to use to make it seem as if they were truly battling me, all of which were alleged to not truly harm me. I had to demonstrate my acting ability and performed a death-scene that would have done Shakespeare proud.

"Not dead," that bossy eldest sister informed me. "If you're dead, then we have to haul your giant dinosaur body off the mountain and pretend to bury it. Just act like you're being horribly injured by the spells, then Sylvie will pretend banish you."

"And then what? I pretend disappear?"

"No, actually disappear, then reappear at Sylvie's house." She frowned. "You can do that, right?"

I could, but thought for a moment about denying the ability, just to annoy this witch. I decided against it since being dragged through the woods while I played dead was probably plan B and I didn't like that idea at all.

"Yep, I can do that."

The twin looked at her watch. "You'd better get moving."

Sylvie walked over to me, wrapping her arms around my waist and pulling me in for a long passionate kiss. "Be careful. I'll see you at home after this is all over."

Home. Not "my house." And she'd kissed me right in front of her sisters. Oh, the things I was going to do to her once we were "home."

"Another kiss for luck?" I asked. It was a request she granted with a smile. Then she spun me around, swatted me on my ass, and told me to get going.

I got up to Clinton's compound with plenty of time to spare, so I amused myself by sneaking up on some of the houses and peeking in their windows, trying to get an idea of which ones I'd be able to stomp on without getting too many splinters in my feet. At midnight on the dot, I scooted a hundred feet or so down the road and transformed into a T-rex.

It had been a long time since I'd either seen a real T-rex or the *Jurassic Park* movies, so I decided to embellish a bit on my recollections. Sixty feet long ought to do it. Red and black, because those were my favorite colors. And feathers, because feathers are fabulous. Everyone knows that.

Done, I let out a huge roar and laughed when three were-wolf guards screamed and fell out of some nearby trees. A giant dinosaur laughing frightened them just as much as my roar, and they took off, shouting the alarm. I followed, kicking over a few trees along the way for good measure and giving a few more roars just to alert everyone that they needed to get out of the houses I was about to squash.

I'll give these werewolves one thing, they were prepared. I'd barely made it twenty strides before the woods erupted with them and they began to shoot at me. I don't care what that eldest sister witch said. It hurt. I bled. And it was then that I decided that I needed to change the script. There was no way I was going to keep marching through a hailstorm of bullets just to smash a few houses, then turn around and head back the other way. Screw the houses. I'd just knock over a few more trees and call it done.

And hadn't that eldest sister witch said something about fire? Yes, I distinctly remembered her saying that I should burn the forest down. It seemed a bit excessive, but I was never one to say "no" to excess, so fire it was.

I spun around, sending a few werewolves flying with my tail as I karate-kicked a few trees down and began to run back down the road—careful not to run so fast that I lost my pursuers, but definitely fast enough that they had a hard time shooting me. Every so often I'd turn to the side and shoot flames out my mouth, setting nearby bushes and trees on fire. I could tell when the werewolves realized where I was heading because a few of them shapeshifted into their wolf forms and raced around me through the woods, getting ahead no doubt to warn the others that I was coming.

By the time I'd arrived, there was a nice plume of black smoke behind me from where I'd set some foliage on fire. The other werewolves immediately attacked, and I was trapped between the two groups, getting shot at and jumped on by four-legged werewolves who were hanging off me by some very sharp teeth and claws.

It hurt. It hurt a whole lot, and I wasn't exactly having fun anymore. My pretty feathers were torn, my leathery skin was marred with bullet holes and bite marks. The witches were nowhere in sight yet, and I really didn't want to endure much more of this while I waited for them to show up. I'd do a lot of things for my couch-witch, but I was giving her and her sisters five minutes to get their butts up here or I was ditching this plan for something less painful.

Somehow, I managed to continue moving forward in spite of every effort by about a hundred werewolves to kill me. Once inside the compound, I got to work knocking down some houses and setting fire to a few just to be thorough about it.

Thankfully the witches arrived just before I'd run out of houses to smash and burn. That eldest sister witch was a very good actress because I completely believed she was furiously angry. She yelled something very rude at me, then began putting out the fires I'd worked so hard to create. The others began to cast their fake magical spells, and I remembered just in time that I needed to pretend to be injured by them.

Pretending to be injured wasn't exactly a stretch since I'd been shot and chewed on extensively. I staggered around, clutching my chest with one hand and waving the other about as if I were trying to ward off the spell effects. Sylvie raced toward me, and, overcome with joy, I forgot my role for a moment and picked her up, bringing her up to my face so I could kiss her.

Except I couldn't really kiss her because like this I was big enough to fit her whole head in my mouth. Actually, I could fit her whole body in my mouth. I don't think she would have liked that, though, so instead of shoving her in my mouth, I just nuzzled her.

"Stop. You're supposed to be ferocious," she whispered. Then she made it worse by booping me on the nose.

"Are you ready?" she asked.

Was I ready? I was shot and bit and clawed and was pretty sure I had splinters in both feet and my tail. I wanted nothing more than to change back into my regular form and go home —to our home—and wait for my couch-witch to return.

I nodded and she pulled one of the spent button charms from her pocket, tossing it at me. I caught it with my other hand and groaned dramatically, setting her down before staggering around a bit and falling to the ground in a heap.

Oh, crap. That's right. I wasn't supposed to die; I was just supposed to disappear. Oh, well, I guess a dead dinosaur could vanish just as easily as a live one. I opened one eye to see Sylvie waving frantically at me, mouthing "go, go."

Giving her a wink, I left that mountainside and appeared in front of our home, scaring the crap out of a goblin walking a pair of groundhogs on leashes down the sidewalk.

Home. I walked up the steps to the porch, let myself in, and smiled. Home. Well, it would be home as soon as Sylvie was here with me.

CHAPTER 21

SYLVIE

*W*e stood in the charred remains of Dallas's compound, bits of the forest still smoking. I cringed, avoiding Cassie's eyes, knowing that this was far more damage than she'd wanted Eshu to do. So many people had lost their homes, but Eshu had kept to the part of the deal that said he wasn't supposed to harm or kill anyone. Outside of some singed fur, none of the werewolves were hurt. And I couldn't exactly blame Eshu for roaring fire when the werewolves had riddled him with bullet holes and been hanging off him by their claws and fangs.

The good thing that came from all this was that the werewolves were not only grateful to us for helping with the fight, they owed Lucien big-time for putting out the fires in the forest as well as Cassie for putting out the ones in the compound. And I had no doubt that everyone in the town would offer to come up and help them rebuild, further cementing a new relationship between the werewolves and the other beings of Accident.

Dallas came forward, his silver hair full of soot, the burns on his hands already healing. "Thank you. Thank you,

Perkins witches and demon mates for seeing the fire on the mountain and coming to our rescue. I am in your debt. And you." He turned to Clinton. "My son who disgraced himself by refusing to challenge me, by turning traitor and cowardly sneaking away with a group of other traitors to steal part of our territory. You had every advantage here. You could have watched the monster kill us and burn us and been in a position to take the entire mountain as the new pack alpha."

"Wasn't gonna let a giant lizard destroy the home I grew up in or watch idly while he killed wolves I always considered my friends and family," Clinton said with a gruff note in his voice. "Couldn't stand by and let my father fight without me by his side."

Dallas clapped his son on the shoulder. "I want to offer reconciliation. Come back to the pack, and all will be forgiven. You'll be my son once more, and your followers will be welcome back with no penalties."

I saw the doubt in Clinton's eyes and knew what he wanted. He'd been an alpha. He'd had his own pack. It would be impossible for him to go back now and be happy.

"Let's negotiate this in my office tomorrow morning." I stepped forward and put a hand on each werewolf's arm. "Just the two of you, with me as a witness. This is a family matter. You should both discuss this in private, then make a joint announcement to both groups of werewolves."

Clinton nodded. "I like that idea. How about you, Da?"

Dallas thought for a moment, then nodded as well. "Yeah. There are details to work out that should be private to our family—just the two of us. And Sylvie as witness, of course."

Cassie came forward at that. "Then let's all head back to our homes for the night. Dallas, once you've assessed the damage, any displaced wolves are welcome to stay in Accident until there are suitable accommodations up here for them. I can ask Hollister to use his hotel, and several of us in town are set up for guests."

Clinton held up a hand. "We've got room at our place as well. None of our houses got damaged, and everyone's got a spare room or bed for anyone who needs a temporary spot to den down."

Cassie smiled over at him, then looked back to Dallas. "Of course we'll help you rebuild as well. I'll put out the call, and by tomorrow noon we can have a crew up here with supplies helping to put up new homes and whatever else you need."

Dallas lowered his head, but not before I saw the sparkle of what I was pretty sure were tears in his eyes. By the time he looked up, they were gone.

"I appreciate that, Cassie." He reached out and patted her shoulder, sliding his hand down to brush against the side of her boob.

Some things might change, but some things would always remain the same—like Dallas being a letch. I looked over and saw Tink glaring at him and realized he was really going to get an earful and maybe more tonight. Then I remembered what she'd told me and wondered if that wasn't his intention all along.

We all piled in our cars, following Cassie and Lucien as we drove down the mountain and back to town. I was covered in soot, smelled like smoke, was tired and sore—but I was happy. Eshu was right. Things had somehow ended where they were supposed to in spite of the convoluted path they'd taken. I just had to make sure the negotiations tomorrow went the way I wanted them to go, then we could all rest easy that there was peace among the werewolves.

But first I needed a shower, and then I planned on curling up in bed with my sexy not-a-demon, who hopefully was no longer a fire-spewing oversized T-rex.

CHAPTER 22

"*I* can't rejoin the pack, Da. I want to lead, and I want to run a pack with different rules."

Clinton had said this same thing on Monday, but this time it was said with a pleading instead of demanding tone of voice. He wanted his father to understand. And he truly wanted his blessing on this.

"Why can't you just come back? We'll work on those things you talked about, and I can give you some added responsibilities."

Dallas went on to suggest different things Clinton could be in charge of, while I sat back and just listened. If either one realized we were behind the giant fire-breathing dinosaur, neither mentioned it. As expected, the town had rallied to the cause. Some had made early morning trips to bring lumber and building supplies from stores on the other side of the wards, and there was now the equivalent of a barn raising going on up on Heartbreak Mountain. All of Accident's diverse residents were chipping in, some helping build, others providing food, and others organizing clothing and household supply drives to replace what had been lost.

We were all coming together as a community, and I had high hopes for the future of werewolves in our town.

If only these two stubborn Dickskin men could agree, that is.

"I'm not rejoining the pack," Clinton said with a bit more firmness. "It's not going to happen."

There was silence, and I held my breath, worried that this whole thing was going to unravel, and we'd be back where we started.

Dallas sighed, running a hand through his silver hair. "Okay. I'll accept that you've got your own pack. I'll even let anyone in my pack go join yours without penalty, but you can't stay on the mountain."

That was huge. Huge. But Clinton didn't see it that way.

"I can't take my pack outside the wards and have any kind of life," Clinton protested. "Exile isn't any kind of compromise."

Dallas waved his hands. "I don't mean exile. Your pack can stay in Accident, just not on Heartbreak Mountain. I got money set aside for you, plus you got what your mother left for you. Buy a few acres and start somewhere else inside the wards. I hear there's land to the east for sale."

"The marshes?" Clinton scoffed. "And how the hell am I gonna establish a pack on two acres? That's not enough to build on, let alone anywhere to run or hunt."

"There's some land on Savior Mountain," I told the pair. "The wards encompass about fifty acres up there that no one's owned since that group of elves left twenty years ago."

"There." Dallas nodded. "You could have your pack there. Fifty acres is a decent size."

"You've got thousands of acres," Clinton countered. "And yeah, fifty might be enough to have a compound, a small bit of livestock and a few gardens, but not enough for any sort of hunting."

"I want this to work, Clinton, really I do, but I can't allow your pack to take a portion of our territory. I can welcome you back, or I can give your new pack my blessing if they're set up elsewhere, but I can't split off part of our pack's lands. They're not mine; they belong to the pack. They belong to all the werewolves, and they've been pack lands for two hundred years. I can't start dividing things up because my son wants to go off on his own."

I blinked, suddenly realizing Dallas's position. I'd been thinking he was just being greedy and stubborn, not wanting to share his mountain with his son, but now I understood.

And now that I understood, I had an idea.

"Heartbreak Mountain belongs to all the werewolves of the pack." I waited for Dallas's nod. "And that includes Clinton and the wolves that follow him. They're part of the original pack, so they should have an ownership interest in the mountain as well."

"They do, but I can't start splitting up the mountain," Dallas argued. "It sets a precedent. The territory belongs to all the werewolves as a group, not each one individually owning a few acres."

I nodded. "I get it. Just hear me out a minute here. What if a portion of Heartbreak Mountain could be designated as protected land—as land that all werewolves in Accident regardless of pack have an equal claim to. It could be a sort of preserve that is open to all werewolves during the full moon," I suggested. "Clinton can establish his pack elsewhere, but during the moon, you all can come together to hunt on land that's set aside as a werewolf national park."

Dallas screwed up his face as if I'd just forced him to eat a lemon, but Clinton appeared interested in the idea.

"It would heal a lot of wounds, Da," he said. "Us all coming together each full moon, just like old times, hunting on the land our ancestors have hunted on for hundreds of years, keeping the traditions and the old ways. Each month we'd be remembering where we came from and giving thanks to those who took a chance on a bunch of witches and made the mountain their home."

It was the most stirring speech I'd ever heard from Clinton. I felt so proud of him, knowing how far he'd come in just a few months from the angry, rebellious, asshole of a werewolf he'd been to a leader of his pack.

"Okay, but our pack gifts it to conservation," Dallas stated. "There's a ceremony, and it's very clear that my pack is the one that is gifting this land in honor of our traditions and past."

"You get all the glory," I agreed. "But I'm letting you know right now that gifting a portion of the mountain into conservatory means it's open to *all* werewolves. It's a place where they can all come during the full moon and hunt, regardless of what pack they belong to…. regardless of whether they're with a pack or are a lone wolf. You must welcome Shelby and Stanley there during the full moon as well. I don't care if you speak to them at all the rest of the month, but during the full moon, all differences will be put aside, and werewolves will come together in peace and fellowship to honor their past and their traditions."

Even the mention of Shelby and Stanley didn't dim the gleam that had come into both werewolves' eyes. Dallas was imagining the glory. Clinton was seeing a glimmer of hope that his pack could be allowed to thrive and not be completely isolated.

"We will assist Clinton in buying the land for his pack," I told them, "but I need to ask that you give them two months to begin building."

A shadow crossed Dallas's face. "Everyone is going to think I'm weak."

"He helped the pack when he didn't have to. He sent

scouts ahead to warn you all that a monster was coming. He and his wolves slowed the attacker down and gave you time to ready yourselves. They stayed and helped you fight. They offered to house your displaced people, to help you rebuild." I held out my hands. "I don't think anyone would believe you weak for giving them a few months to make the transition."

Dallas nodded. "Guessing you're right. Okay, I'll do it."

"Two months." Clinton frowned. "I'll do my best, but is there room for an extension if we can't quite get the place bought and moved out by then?"

"As long as you don't take two years, I might be a bit reasonable," Dallas drawled.

"And when it's not the full moon?" I asked. "It's going to be hard on folk if they're forbidden to talk to or even look at each other most of the month, then make nice for three days."

"If I'm forgiving Clinton, then I can't demand others do different," Dallas admitted. "I'm thinking each werewolf needs to make their own decisions on whether they feel it's right to socialize with wolves of another pack or those who are lone wolves. No matter what they decide, I'll make sure my people know they gotta be polite and welcoming during the moon, though. Best behavior. Treating all werewolves like guests during the full moon, even if they still hate someone's guts."

I guess that was as good as it was going to get for the time being.

"Then let's seal this as a vow," I told them, pulling a paper out of my notebook. I'd jotted down what the pair had agreed upon as a sort of contract. It might not look too professional, but if a handwritten note worked for Temperance Perkins and the others who'd originally made up the town of Accident, then it would work for us.

Dallas and Clinton both read over my chicken scratching,

then took out pocket knives, jabbing themselves in the thumb and making a blood-print next to their names. I signed my name in a more traditional manner, with an ink pen, then informed both of them that I'd have copies delivered by this evening.

We had a deal. We had peace. And all it had taken was a little bit of deception and theatrics on our part. There was still a lot that needed to happen to make sure that things went smoothly between the two packs, but I was giddy with excitement over what had been accomplished here today.

Clinton had his pack. Dallas had his pride. And Shelby and Stanley would have the opportunity to socialize with other wolves as well as hunt together on the lands they'd grown up on.

I left the meeting and walked back to my house, and for the very first time since I'd died, I didn't feel drained or tired.

I was good. I was more than good. Healing. Happy. Falling in love with a sexy demon who made me laugh and rocked my world. I picked up the phone and called over to the diner to order some carry-out and looked up as I heard my front door open.

There stood Eshu, a bottle of wine in one hand and a pizza in the other. Beside him was a bottle of rum and a box from the butcher shop that I would bet contained a quarter of beef.

"Better put that in the freezer before it thaws," I told him.

"Later." He leaned forward and kissed me. "First we celebrate with rum and wine and pizza. Then sex."

"How about sex first, so I'm actually sober?" I laughed.

He set down the wine, put the pizza box on top of the meat box, and gathered me into his arms. "A much better idea, my brilliant, beloved couch-witch. Come with me to bed. Or to the couch. Your choice."

I laughed, grabbed his hand, and hauled him off to my bedroom.

Life was good. Life was more than good. And I only had to die to realize it.

* * *

WANT to know what's up next? About contests and give-aways? What I'm reading and recommend? Glimpses into my life and writing process and more? Subscribe to my news-letter at: DebraDunbar.com

All the fiendish fun, and none of the spam!

* * *

IMP WORLD NOVELS

The Imp Series
A Demon Bound

Satan's Sword

Elven Blood

Devil's Paw

Imp Forsaken

Angel of Chaos

Kingdom of Lies

Exodus

Queen of the Damned

The Morning Star

* * *

Half-breed Series
Demons of Desire

Sins of the Flesh

Cornucopia

Unholy Pleasures

City of Lust

* * *

Imp World Novels
No Man's Land

Stolen Souls

Three Wishes

Northern Lights

Far From Center

Penance

* * *

<u>Northern Wolves</u>

Juneau to Kenai

Rogue

Winter Fae

Bad Seed

ACKNOWLEDGMENTS

Thanks to my copyeditors Erin Zarro and Jennifer Cosham whose eagle eyes catch all the typos and keep my comma problem in line, and to Renee George for cover design.

ABOUT THE AUTHOR

Debra lives in a little house in the woods of Maryland with her sons and two slobbery bloodhounds. On a good day, she jogs and horseback rides, hopefully managing to keep the horse between herself and the ground. Her only known super power is 'Identify Roadkill'.

For more information:
www.debradunbar.com
Debra Dunbar's Author page